T0193616

STRAIGHT FROM THE HEART

A CHILD'S JOURNEY TO LOVE AND BE LOVED

Muriel Kennedy, PhD

WESTBOW
PRESS®
A DIVISION OF THOMAS NELSON
& ZONDERVAN

WestBow Press books may be ordered through booksellers or by contacting:

WestBow Press
A Division of Thomas Nelson & Zondervan
1663 Liberty Drive
Bloomington, IN 47403
www.westbowpress.com
1 (866) 928-1240

Quote by Martin Luther King, Jr. reprinted by arrangement with The Heirs to the Estate of Martin Luther King Jr., c/o Writers House as agent for the proprietor New York, NY.

ISBN: 978-1-9736-1632-0 (sc)
ISBN: 978-1-9736-1633-7 (hc)
ISBN: 978-1-9736-1631-3 (e)

Library of Congress Control Number: 2018901018

Print information available on the last page.

WestBow Press rev. date: 9/05/2018

Dedication

Straight from the Heart: A Child's Journey to Love and Be Loved is dedicated to parents who have remained committed to loving and caring for their children while enduring challenges related to divorce, separation, abandonment, homelessness, chronic substance abuse, and/or domestic violence. This novel is designed to serve as a source of motivation, inspiration, and encouragement to you and your family, as you remain committed to loving yourself and the children that God has entrusted into your care.

Contents

upon reading and/or literature based. Given my strengths in math and science, I decided to major in mechanical engineering.

I would not have pursued a degree in engineering if I had not been told by my ninth-grade Algebra 1 teacher, Mrs. Edith Gregg, that I had what it took to become an engineer. She subsequently encouraged me to sign up for geometry and Algebra 2 in tenth grade so that I would be able to take Algebra 3 the following year and Calculus I during my senior year in high school. I looked up to Mrs. Gregg—and I did exactly what she said I could. I believed in her and trusted her judgment. I am extremely blessed to have had an Algebra 1 teacher who believed in me and focused on my strengths in math and science. These strengths allowed me to compensate for my challenges with reading while I developed confidence in my ability to succeed at whatever I put my mind to.

In understanding my own struggles with reading, I set out to write a book trilogy that would be highly stimulating, educational, instructive, motivational and, above all, engaging and fun to read—especially for youth and adults who might have a learning disability and/or struggle with reading. I personally know how good it feels to be able to read a book in its entirety, from cover to cover. It gives you a sense of accomplishment and actually makes you feel good about yourself, knowing you have done something that the average American might do on a frequent basis with admirable ease. Because my ninth grade Algebra 1 teacher chose to focus on my strengths, while simultaneously helping me to overcome my challenges, I tend to do the same with the children, youth, and families that I have been blessed to work with over the years, as a licensed clinical psychologist. Yes, I changed my career field from mechanical engineering to clinical psychology. After working for three years as an engineer, I decided to pursue my Master of Science and Doctor of Philosophy degrees in clinical psychology, which is a testimony in and of itself.

In appreciating the importance of believing in oneself and not giving up on one's hopes and dreams, I wanted to share the motivation for writing the Jamaal series. In this series, the complexity of relationships is explored through the heart and eyes of Jamaal; his best friend, Trevon; his estranged father, James; his deeply devoted mother, Marlene; and his very loving and caring grandmother, Irene. I hope that caring adults will be inspired to continue believing in their ability to make a difference in the lives of our youth. For our beloved youth truly are our future leaders and our most valuable resource. In closing, I must caution that the story of Jamaal will undoubtedly stir up emotions. It also will serve as a true source of motivation, inspiration, and encouragement to children, youth, and families that have sustained a significant loss due to an untimely death, separation, divorce, and/or abandonment. So, I strongly recommend that you keep a box of Kleenex within arm's reach and hold on to your indelible faith, as Jamaal takes you on his heartrending journey to love and be loved.

ACKNOWLEDGMENTS

The Lord truly is the joy and the strength of my life, and I would like to thank Him for blessing me with the ability to love and accept myself and others unconditionally. I also thank Him for blessing me with the dynamic gift of creative writing. It is a gift that I pray will continue to be used for His honor and His glory, as lives are transformed and made whole. Secondly, I would like to thank my beloved biological and spiritual family, which consists of persons that I have been blessed to meet and come to know and love over the years. I love meeting people and making new friends, and I can honestly say that God has blessed me to know and be influenced by some of the most wonderful and truly amazing, spirit-filled individuals. I value you and your friendship, and I thank you for believing in me and valuing the work that God has entrusted unto me. Your unwavering support motivates and inspires me!

Next, I would like to thank God for the very special teachers, professors, instructors, and mentors that He has placed in my life over the years. Having truly devoted people like this in life is a tremendous gift, and I would hate to think where our nation would be without them. The field of teaching is said to be a thankless profession, and persons who have committed their lives to teaching and educating others may never know the impact they have made on our lives unless we take the time to personally tell them. Should *you* take the time to let *a teacher* know how she/he has made a difference in *your* life, I am sure that she/he will be quite pleased that you did. And you never know, you might be the one to serve as a source of motivation and inspiration in strengthening that teacher's resolve to continue teaching for another twenty to thirty years.

Lastly, I would like to thank the youth, young adults, and families that I have been blessed to work with throughout my career as a licensed clinical psychologist. Your individual and collective strengths in overcoming some of life's greatest challenges serve as a source of motivation and inspiration for the work that I do. In turn, you keep me inspired, motivated, and deeply committed to the field of clinical psychology: a field and profession that is directly linked to my higher calling, mission, and ministry—which is indeed a blessing.

I sincerely thank each of you for your interest in the Jamaal series, and I pray that God will continue to bless and keep you and your loved ones, now and forevermore.

My Sister, My Brother

My sister, my brother,
Can we truly love one another?

Yes, we may fuss,
And we may also fight,
But in the middle of the night
Are we still precious in each other's sight?

My sister, my brother,
Are you willing to lend a hand
To help a fellow woman or fellow man?

My sister, my brother,
My love for you
Is oh, so true;
So, with that knowledge,
What are you gonna do?

My sister, my brother,
Your love for me
Is far deeper than the eye can see,
And, I thank you,
My sister, my brother,
For allowing me
To be me.

Although we may fuss,
And sometimes fight,
We will always be precious
In each other's sight;
Because, you see,
My sister, my brother,
We truly do love one another.

—Muriel Kennedy

CHAPTER 1

WHAT IS LOVING DISCIPLINE?
A MOTHER'S STORY

Keyana is a vivacious little ten-year-old girl who doesn't seem to have a care in the world. She has smooth brown skin, curly black hair, hazel-brown eyes, and a deep dimple in her right cheek. Without an older sister to look up to or a younger brother to boss around, Keyana often spends time alone in her room, reading her favorite picture books while playing make-believe with her multiethnic dolls. She also delights in watching classic episodes of *Sesame Street* and *The Electric Company*. She even occasionally spends time watching reruns of sitcoms like *The Brady Bunch, Good Times,* and *Family Affair.*

On this particular afternoon, Keyana is joyfully playing with her Christie doll as the theme song to *Good Times* grabs her attention. She is filled with glee and excitement as she leaps from her bed onto the floor. She rhythmically sings along while twirling around in circles, with her Christie doll flying in the air. She is desperately hoping that the episode will feature her favorite child actor, Penny. As the theme song comes to an end, Keyana hops up on the bed, places the remote control next to her, and lovingly cradles her Christie doll in her arms as she settles in to watch the show.

Keyana is engrossed in the episode of *Good Times* in which the biological mother becomes upset with her young daughter, Penny, causing the daughter to run away from home. "Oh my!" Keyana anxiously cries out as she thinks to herself, *Is Penny going to be okay? Who will she stay with? Will she come back home?* Deeply troubled by the thought of Penny running away from home, Keyana abruptly places her Christie doll onto the bed, grabs the remote control, and turns the television off. She then leaps to her feet, races out of the room, and dashes downstairs in search of her mother.

As she turns toward the kitchen, Keyana hears the remix of a song that was made popular by the group Arrested Development. The song captures her attention as she stops at the kitchen doorway and peers in.

Keyana notices her mother swaying from side to side to the rhythm of the music. She stands silently at the door, admiring her mother as she hums and sings along to the song while preparing dinner. Keyana smiles as she thinks to herself, *I'm going to be just like my mother when I grow up.* She lets out a calming sigh as she takes in the aroma of her mother's Cajun-style food. There is home-cooked jambalaya in the pot next to the cilantro lime rice. Keyana loves to watch her mother as she cooks, her dark brown skin glistening from the heat in the kitchen, giving her a glow Keyana loves to see. Keyana shakes her head from side to side as she thinks to herself, *How could Penny's mother be so mean to her and cause her to run away from home?*

Keyana's mother, Kiarra, is caught off guard as she turns and sees Keyana standing in the doorway. *I know that look,* she thinks to herself, while calmly asking, "What is it, dear? Are you okay? Is there something bothering you?" Kiarra can tell that Keyana is deeply troubled by something, but she is not quite sure what. She stops what she is doing, turns the music down, and locks eyes with her daughter while waiting for her to reply.

Keyana remains silent as she warmly stares into her mother's dark-brown eyes. There is a pensive look on her face.

"Come here, sweetheart," says Kiarra as she beckons to her daughter. "What's the matter?"

Keyana remains silent.

"Come here," Kiarra insists as she reaches out to Keyana.

Keyana drops her head while slowly walking toward her mother. She thinks about the episode of *Good Times* as she looks up at her mother and softly asks, "Mommy, do you love me?"

"Yes, my precious daughter. Of course I love you! In fact, I love you more than you could ever imagine." Kiarra is taken aback by Keyana's question. She cannot imagine what could possibly have caused her daughter to question her love. She reaches out to embrace her. She kisses Keyana on the forehead as she guides her into the family room, where they are able to sit comfortably on the couch to talk.

In experiencing the genuine love that her mother has for her, Keyana continues to think about the episode of *Good Times* and the harsh manner in which the mother treated her young daughter. "Well, Mommy, if you love me, why do you punish me? And why do parents punish their children?"

Kiarra is speechless, wondering what in the world could be causing her daughter to question her love for her. She softly states under her breath, "When was the last time I punished her?" She lets out a deep sigh as she thinks to herself, *Now, how can I explain why parents punish their children in a way that Keyana will understand?*

Keyana pensively stares at the floor and remains silent as she continues to think about Penny and the harsh manner in which her mother treated her.

"Aha," Kiarra whispers under her breath, "I can share the story of Jamaal." She is convinced that Keyana will have a better understanding of why parents punish their children after hearing the story of Jamaal and his family, a family that Kiarra knows very well.

Keyana is sitting quietly next to her mother, pensively twiddling her thumbs.

"My dear child," Kiarra lovingly begins. "Let me tell you a little story about love and discipline and why I punish you in the manner in which I do." Kiarra pulls Keyana tightly to her side as she begins to share the story of Jamaal's heartrending journey to love and be loved: "Once upon a time, there was a little boy named Jamaal. Jamaal was the son of two very, very hardworking parents. His parents loved him dearly. However, when he was four years old, his parents got divorced. Jamaal's father was very active in his life for the first four years following the divorce, but he gradually stopped spending as much time with Jamaal for various reasons. As a result, Jamaal was raised by his mother, who loved him dearly."

Kiarra pauses as she glances at Keyana and notices her bright, sparkling eyes staring up at her. She leans in and kisses Keyana on the forehead. "Just as I love you," she states lovingly.

Keyana blushes as her mother warmly embraces her, while redirecting her attention back to the story.

"Now, where was I?" Kiarra asks with a smile.

"You were talking about how much Jamaal's mother loved him," Keyana exclaims with glee as she bounces up and down on the couch.

"Yes, I was sharing how Jamaal's mother loved him dearly, just as I love you. She wanted to give him *everything* his little heart desired. You see, Jamaal's mother grew up in a single-parent household, and she did not want to see Jamaal go through the same hardships she had to go through. She also felt guilty about the divorce and the impact that the divorce would have on her son—"

Keyana interrupts, letting her curiosity get the best of her. "Mommy, did Jamaal have any brothers and sisters?"

"No, sweetheart, Jamaal was an only child. However, his mother was very concerned about him being a young African American male who would have to grow up in a society that she did not feel valued black males and all they have to offer." Kiarra pauses as she thinks about how things have drastically changed over the years. "Since she thought the outside world would be hard on him, she wanted to make things as easy as possible for him at home. Therefore, she did not discipline Jamaal, because she did not want to be *too hard* on him. She thought that he had it bad enough being a black male growing up in what can be a very mean and cruel world. So whatever Jamaal wanted, he got. Wherever Jamaal wanted to go, he went. Whenever he wanted to hang out with his friends, his mother allowed him to do so. Whenever he wanted money, she gave it to him. Jamaal got everything his little heart desired, and I do mean *everything*."

"Wow! That sure sounds like fun. I wish Jamaal's mother was my mother," Keyana exuberantly states with a broad smile on her face.

Kiarra smiles as she playfully pulls Keyana tightly to her side. "Yes, that made Jamaal very happy, especially when he was young and was able to get his way. He was the apple of his mother's eye. Jamaal's mother thought that she was doing right by him in allowing him to have his way. She also thought that she was demonstrating to him how much she truly loved him. However, as Jamaal began school and grew older, he became more and more confused by the way he was treated at home versus the way he was treated in school. The teachers did not treat him in the same manner as his mother did. When he went to school, he expected to get his way with his friends as well as his teachers. Needless to say, he was not given the same attention from his peers and teachers that he had become accustomed to getting at home."

"Wow, that must have made Jamaal feel sad!" Keyana exclaims in amazement.

"Yes, I am sure that did make Jamaal feel very sad," Keyana's mother replies. "However, he was not able to express his sadness to his teachers or his mother. So he started acting out in class and also at home, and over time his sadness turned to anger. Jamaal seemed to be angry at everything and everybody, including his father, who was not there for him in the way that Jamaal felt he should have been."

Keyana remains deeply engrossed in the story of Jamaal, keeping her eyes fixed on her mother.

"You see, Jamaal expected the world to revolve around him, because he was used to being the center of attention at home. Jamaal was, and still is, his mother's pride and joy. When Jamaal turned ten, he rebelled against his teacher and would get into fights constantly with his classmates. As a result, Jamaal was suspended from school several times throughout the school year, and he eventually began to rebel against his mother as well."

Keyana gently taps her mother on the arm while solemnly asking, "Did Jamaal fight with his mother?"

"Sad to say, he did. Jamaal and his mother bickered and argued constantly when he turned eleven, yet his mother continued to be there for him. And thank God no one got hurt."

Keyana's eyes widen as she exclaims, "Yes, that is good." She is relieved to know that Jamaal's mother did not give up on him and that no one got hurt. She smiles with relief, as she leans her head to the side and looks up at her mother with great love and admiration.

Kiarra thinks about how much she loves her daughter as she continues to share the story of Jamaal: "Over time, Jamaal began to resent his mother. He would take his anger out on her, because he felt that she had set him up to be let down by other people, those he expected to embrace him and allow him to have his way. His mother then stopped giving him the things that she had been giving him, because of his behavior and because she could no longer afford the expensive items Jamaal insisted on having. The disappointment that Jamaal experienced at home greatly contributed to the anger and resentment he felt toward his mother. His anger escalated to the point where the police had to be called, due to repeated threats by Jamaal to run away from home and/or cause harm to himself. All this was out of anger and resentment toward his mother."

Keyana warmly gazes at her mother as she begins to think about the episode of *Good Times* that she had seen earlier. She is anxious to know how the story of Jamaal will end and remains deeply captivated by the intriguing nature of the story.

"Jamaal and his mother began to grow further and further apart, and she was no longer able to communicate her love to him." Kiarra pauses as she notices Keyana intently staring up at her. She leans down and kisses her on the top of her head while emphatically stating, "And, sweetheart, without communication it is hard to express and show love. However, Jamaal's mother thought that she had demonstrated how much she loved him by giving him material things and the freedom to do as he pleased. And she gradually became more and more depressed as he continued to rebel against everything and everybody. Jamaal's acting-out behavior hurt his mother deeply, and she did not know what to do."

"Mommy, what did Jamaal's mother do?" Keyana inquisitively asks as she continues to think about the episode of *Good Times*.

"Well, by this time, Jamaal was at risk of failing the sixth grade. He made straight A grades when he was in the first, second, and third grade. Then he began to make Bs and Cs in the fourth and fifth grade. However, in the sixth grade, he made nothing but Fs, and there was talk about placing him in a special school for kids with 'serious emotional problems.' Given Jamaal's mother's depression, she began to feel helpless and hopeless, and she unwittingly caused Jamaal's acting-out behavior to increase by constantly telling him that he had a serious emotional problem and would not amount to anything."

Keyana begins to feel compassion for Jamaal while remaining deeply intrigued by the story.

Kiarra is hoping that the story of Jamaal will help Keyana understand the importance of effective communication, love, and discipline. She continues to share. "As a result, Jamaal began to view himself as a 'problem child,' and he started ignoring his mother, which made it that much more difficult for her to communicate with him. He then began hanging out with other so-called 'troubled youth,' and he ended up developing a special friendship with a fifteen-year-old male named Trevon. There was a special bond between Jamaal and Trevon. Considering their relationship, Trevon was quick to introduce Jamaal to a group of his peers, which consisted of thirteen-, fourteen-, and fifteen-year-old males who were convinced that they would not live to see their sixteenth birthday."

Keyana is listening intently to her mother, and she wonders to herself, *What could have possibly caused them to think that they would not live to see their sixteenth birthdays?*

Kiarra looks down at her watch and realizes that she needs to finish preparing dinner. She is surprised by how much time has passed. She turns to her daughter and gives her a hug. "Well, dear, I am going to have to end the story *here* for now," she lovingly states. "I will finish the story about Jamaal after we say our prayers and I tuck you in for bed tonight."

Keyana abruptly cries out, "No, Mommy! No-o-o-o-o-o-o! I want to hear the rest of the story!" She leaps to her feet and passionately pleads with her mother while frantically stomping her feet on the floor. "Mommy, ple-e-e-e-e-ease! I want to hear the rest of the story. I want to know what happened to Jamaal and his mother. Ple-e-e-e-e-ease, Mommy! Ple-e-e-e-e-ease!" Keyana begins to tug at her mother's arm while continuing to plead with her.

Kiarra realizes that her daughter is desperately attempting to get her to give in. She can appreciate that Keyana wants to hear the rest of the story as she inwardly smiles at her objectionable reaction. Kiarra firmly looks her daughter in the eyes while stating softly, yet firmly, "Now, Keyana, I know that you want to hear the rest of the story, and I wish I could finish telling it to you. But we are going to have to pause here for now, because you have to start your homework, and I have to finish cooking dinner. The Martins will be joining us for dinner, in celebration of life, the joy of knowing the Lord, and just being thankful that your father has been blessed to see his fortieth birthday."

Keyana's eyes widen as she exclaims, "The Martins are coming over!"

"Yes, sweetheart, the Martins are coming over."

Keyana begins to jump up and down with glee while enthusiastically asking, "Are Jeanette and Jamie coming too?"

"Yes, Jeanette and Jamie will be coming over as well." Kiarra smiles as she gently wraps her arms around Keyana's waist in an attempt to temper her overly enthusiastic reaction. "Are you happy now?" Kiarra asks while looking her squarely in the eyes.

"Yes, Mommy! I am very happy!" Keyana excitedly replies as she begins to do her happy dance.

Kiarra smiles inwardly and snappily retorts, "Well, that's good. Now go, hurry and finish your homework, because dinner will be ready soon, and I promise I will finish the story about Jamaal and why I punish you as I do."

Keyana scurries down the hall and races up the stairs. Upon

reaching the top of the staircase, she turns and blows her mother a kiss, thinking about how much she loves her mother.

Just as Keyana prepares to go into her room, her mother calls out, "Keyana, dear!"

Keyana stops dead in her tracks and smiles as she turns and looks in her mother's direction. "Yes, Mommy?"

"I love you, sweetheart."

Keyana's smile broadens as she races back downstairs to give her mother a big hug. "I love you too, Mommy." She turns and scurries back upstairs to complete her homework. Keyana is excited about spending time with Jeanette and Jamie.

Kiarra shakes her head from side to side, thinking to herself, *That's my baby girl.* She then begins to wonder what their world will be like five years from now when Keyana turns fifteen.

The family enjoys an exquisite five-course Cajun-inspired dinner and spending a fun-filled evening with the Martins. Later, Kiarra is tucking Keyana into bed and placing her beloved, worn, and tattered Mrs. Beasley doll in bed next to her. Keyana gently wraps her arms around the doll as her mother prepares to resume the story of Jamaal.

Kiarra shares how Jamaal's life drastically shifted once he began middle school and was exposed to many of the things that his mother had tried very hard to shield and protect him from. After sharing how the story of Jamaal ended, Kiarra kisses her daughter on the cheek and prepares to exit the room.

Keyana leans over to kiss her Mrs. Beasley doll good night while gently tucking her under the covers.

Kiarra turns out the lights and wishes them both a good night and sweet dreams.

Keyana is very pleased with the manner in which her mother related her disciplinary practices to the story of Jamaal. And she was especially happy to learn how the story of Jamaal ended.

The story of Jamaal, as shared with Keyana, is depicted in the chapters that follow. In the end, Keyana is able to more fully understand why her mother disciplines her in the manner that she does, and she is quite certain that you, also, will enjoy learning how the story of Jamaal ends. So, she warmly invites you to buckle up, sit back, and relax as Jamaal takes you on his riveting journey to love and be loved.

CHAPTER 2

A BOND BETWEEN FRIENDS

As Jamaal enters middle school, he firmly concludes that he no longer wishes to be let down by adults. He expects them to accept him for who he is, without placing conditions on his dress, actions, and behavior. Jamaal often thinks to himself, *If the adults in my life really loved and cared about me, I wouldn't be hurting so badly and crying all the time.* To avoid dealing with the pain that he is experiencing almost every day, Jamaal begins to hang out with older youths at his school. Trevon is someone Jamaal looks up to and admires. He also is extremely smart and quite popular among his peers. However, he refuses to attend class, and he is repeating the eighth grade for the second time. Nevertheless, Trevon is highly respected by the other boys, and he is someone who Jamaal gravitates toward, looks up to, and wants to emulate.

Trevon sees Jamaal from a distance and cries out, "Hey—yo, Jamaal!"

Jamaal hears Trevon calling and thinks to himself, *Wow, I get to hang out with my man, Tre! Someone who accepts me for who I am.* He then mumbles under his breath, "Maybe today won't be so bad after all," as he rushes over to greet Trevon. "Hey, Trevon! Hey, man, what's up?"

"Good to see you, man," states Trevon as he gives Jamaal a

brotherly hug. Jamaal is someone who Trevon has taken a special interest in and has been keeping an eye on, like a big brother. During his brief interactions with him, Trevon has seen Jamaal becoming increasingly withdrawn, isolated, and depressed over the past couple of weeks. So Trevon figures it is time for him to intervene and do something to lift Jamaal's spirit. He openly shares his thoughts and observations: "Jamaal, man, you know I've been watching you, and I noticed that you seem to be a little down over the past couple of weeks. It almost seems like you just lost your best friend."

Jamaal is taken aback by Trevon's comments, which he knows are true. However, he had no idea that others could pick up on the fact that he had been feeling so hopeless. He drops his head and remains silent.

"Hey, I didn't mean to throw you off. I hope you know that you are always welcome to hang out with me and my peeps."

Jamaal shrugs his shoulders. "Yeah, I know," he states in a solemn but nonchalant manner.

Trevon cares deeply for Jamaal and doesn't like seeing him in a sad and despondent mood. It reminds him too much of his own life and how he often felt when he was Jamaal's age. While looking Jamaal in the eyes, he confidently states, "I tell you what, it sure beats hanging around this joint. Walking around feeling all *sad* and whatnot." Trevon begins to think about how fortunate he is to have people in his life who he can turn to for support when he is feeling down and ready to throw in the towel. His eyes light up as he turns to Jamaal and excitedly states, "As a matter of fact, I'm heading over to meet with the crew in a few. Hey, why don't you join me? You can hang out with me and my boys." For Trevon, hanging with his crew is what keeps him emotionally grounded and motivated to live to see another day.

Jamaal is excited about the idea of spending time with Trevon and his crew, and his mood lifts. He naively inquires about how they will be spending their time. "Yeah, man, I would *love* to hang with you and the crew. But what do you guys do when you get together?"

In realizing that Jamaal has no idea what he and his crew do when they get together, Trevon attempts to protect him from the truth. "Oh, we just get together and chill. You know."

Jamaal looks up at Trevon and hesitantly says, in a naive, yet honest, manner, "No, man, I don't know."

Trevon playfully comments, "Man, you know. Skip class, hang out at the mall, shoot hoops, chill until it's time to go home." Trevon attempts to put Jamaal's mind at ease as he firmly states, "You know the routine." Trevon chuckles as he inwardly reflects on how naive Jamaal appears to be—while secretly he is wishing that he could go back in time to the innocence of his own childhood.

"Oh, okay! I got it," Jamaal excitedly replies. "Sounds like fun to me. *You know I'm down!*"

Trevon's friends are like family, and he is very excited about introducing Jamaal to his running partners. However, given their plans for the evening, Trevon decides that it would be better to hold off on introducing Jamaal to his boys. He looks down at his watch. "Man, I didn't realize how late it was. I almost forgot, I got some business to take care of before meeting with the crew." Trevon pauses as he tries to figure out what would work best in introducing Jamaal to the crew. "Jamaal, man, I'd better get going. But look here, what are you doing tomorrow morning?"

"Man, same ole, same ole! Get up, beef with my mom, ride the bus to school with a bunch of losers. Get sent to the office after being told to stop talking and sit down twenty times by my teacher." Jamaal chuckles as he thinks about school and how his life has been going over the past several months. "You know the routine."

Trevon laughs as he thinks about how he'd had similar thoughts when he was actively attending school. "Yeah, man, I know exactly what you mean. I've been there, done that. It's all too familiar!"

"For real? Man, you're kidding me … right?" Jamaal is surprised to learn that Trevon had a similar experience while attending school.

"No, for real. No joke. I know exactly what you're going through, and my boys and I, we vowed to not deal with being disrespected by no one. And when I say *no one*, I do mean *no one!*" Trevon enthusiastically states. "No parents. No teachers. No principals. Not even the cops. Jamaal, man, when I say no one, I do mean *no one!*"

"Man, you guys must feel good, not having to deal with parents and teachers getting on your case all the time. Trevon, man, I wish I had it like that. *Nobody* would be able to tell me *nothing.*" Jamaal playfully punches Trevon on his right shoulder.

"I know that's right!" Trevon gives Jamaal a high five. "Man, they know not to mess with us, because we don't play. We're not having it."

"You bet!" replies Jamaal as he drops his hand to give Trevon a low five.

"So, are you down or what?"

"Yeah, man, sure thing! You know I'm down."

"Okay, I'll let the boys know that you'll be joining us, and I'll hook up with you in the morning. I'll meet you outside your house around seven forty-five. That's the time you leave for school, right?"

"Yeah, I'll see you at seven forty-five in the morning."

"Sounds like a plan. Looking forward to it."

"Yeah, you bet—me too!"

Trevon jogs to the location where he was scheduled to meet with his crew.

Jamaal remains at the park. He heads home after spending several hours at the park next to the school, shooting hoop and hanging out with the other truant youth from the neighborhood. Jamaal arrives home just before ten o'clock at night. He is confronted by his mother, who has been waiting up for him.

Jamaal's mother, Marlene, has had no idea when he would be arriving home. She hears the door opening and immediately calls out, "Jama-a-a-a-a-a-al! Jama-a-a-a-a-a-al! Jamaal, is that you?"

Jamaal doesn't respond. He is thinking to himself, *What in the world does she want? I ain't got time for this. I got enough on my mind as it is, without her getting on my case. I'm not up for this! Not tonight. Not any night, for that matter.* Jamaal enters the house and attempts to avoid making contact with his mother. He makes his way to the base of the stairs.

"Jama-a-a-a-a-al, where have you been? I've been waiting up *all night* for you!" Marlene cries out while swiftly walking toward him.

Jamaal continues to ignore his mother. He wishes now that he had stayed out overnight.

Marlene positions herself in front of the stairs in an attempt to get Jamaal's attention. "*Jamaal*, you heard me!" she yells out. "I've been worried *sick* about you! And I'm *sick and tired* of you coming in whenever you feel like it, disrespecting me and my house!" She clenches her fists, her anger and frustration beginning to show.

Jamaal rolls his eyes and sucks his teeth, while thinking to himself, *How long do I have to put up with this?*

Marlene positions her body directly in front of Jamaal, looks him squarely in the eyes, and furiously states, "This is going to have to stop, and I mean it!" She sharply raises her hand and places it just above her forehead. "I have had it up to *here* with you!"

Jamaal mumbles under his breath. "Yeah, this sure does need to stop, and I know exactly what to do to put a stop to it." He forces his way past his mother and races up the stairs to his bedroom.

Marlene can sense her increasing frustration and anger with her son. She tries very hard to keep it together while angrily chasing behind him. "Jamaal, what did you say!" she cries out in a loud voice. "Were you mumbling at me under your breath?"

Jamaal is becoming increasingly agitated with his mother. "I tell you what! I ain't got time for this!" Jamaal runs towards his room.

Marlene tries to grab him before he gets to his room and slams and locks the door, but she misses.

Jamaal runs into his room and quickly locks himself inside before his mother reaches the door. He immediately turns his stereo on, while mumbling and complaining about the way his life is going. He makes several comments about his dad not being involved in his life, while inwardly griping about the fact that his mother seems to be on his case constantly, to the point where he cannot stand to be around her.

As the bedroom door slams, Marlene begins to bang on it in desperation. "Jama-a-a-a-a-al! Jama-a-a-a-a-al! You had better unlock this door and come out of that room, right now!" Marlene continues to frantically knock on Jamaal's bedroom door while insisting that he open it.

Jamaal continues to ignore his mother as thoughts of running away from home cross his mind.

Marlene feels increasingly hopeless and helpless as she fights back the tears. "Jamaal, I'm sick and tired of you coming in late at night and ignoring me! I'm tired of you disrespecting me and my house! I'm the mother, and I don't have to take this from you!" She is no longer able to fight back the tears as she continues to bang on Jamaal's door. "Jamaal, you open this door and come out of that room right now! This is my house!" Marlene is unable to control her tears as she drops to her knees. "Lord, please help me! I can't take this anymore!"

Jamaal can hear his mother weeping outside his door. He turns his music up full blast to drown out the distressing sound of her crying. He begins to weep, while he gives serious thought to running away from home as a way of escaping the heartache and pain that he constantly feels.

Marlene begins to cry uncontrollably as she calls out to God: "Lord, help me! Ple-e-e-e-e-ease, Lord—I need you! I don't know what to do. I don't know where to turn. My son is slipping away from me, and I don't know what to do. Lord, please help me! I'm begging You Lord, please! Would somebody please help me? I can't take it anymore!"

As Marlene is crying out to the Lord, the telephone rings. God placed Jamaal's mother in his grandmother's heart about an hour before the grandmother decided that she would make the call. It is getting late, and Marlene's mother, Irene, doesn't want to disturb her and Jamaal by calling so late in the evening. However, Mrs. Irene could sense that something wasn't right, and she decided that it would be best to make the call so that she could put her mind at ease. She listens as the phone rings, hoping that someone will answer. She is thinking to herself that Jamaal and his mother must be sound asleep. Mrs. Irene allows the phone to ring a few more times and then decides that her instincts must have been off. She concludes that everything must be fine with Jamaal and his mother.

Just as Mrs. Irene prepares to hang up, Jamaal's mother races to answer the phone, wiping the tears from her eyes. She faintly says, "Hello?" as she attempts to fight back the tears. She sniffles quietly as she struggles not to break down in tears while on the phone.

In hearing her daughter's voice, Mrs. Irene warmly asks, "Marlene, is that you?"

Marlene is relieved to hear her mother's voice on the other end of the line, as she fights back the tears. "Oh, Momma, it's *so good* to hear your voice. I was starting to feel like I was about to *lose it.*"

"Oh, my dear, what's the matter?"

"Momma, I just can't take it anymore. I feel like I'm about to lose my mind," states Marlene through her tears.

Mrs. Irene sighs while remaining silent.

Marlene remains silent until she regains her composure.

"Marlene, don't tell me it's Jamaal again. Don't tell me the two of you have been going at it again. He's still at it, isn't he?"

"Momma, I don't know what to do! He won't talk to me. He won't listen to a thing I say. He ignores me. He's failing all of his classes. His teachers are constantly calling me at my job. I feel like I'm about to lose my mind *worrying* over that *boy*. I just can't take it anymore. Momma, I have had it—"

Mrs. Irene interrupts, attempting to comfort her daughter. "Now, now, it's going to be okay."

Marlene can feel herself becoming more and more upset as she shares her fears and worries with her mother. "Momma, he comes in late at night wearing those stupid headphones, with his jeans hanging off his *butt*! To tell you the truth, I never know when he's going to come home or if he's coming home at all, for that matter. I'm worried *sick* about him, and I don't know what to do!"

"I understand your concerns, dear—"

"But Ma, I feel like I'm losing my son! And I'm so afraid that he's going to end up with the wrong crowd and end up getting himself killed. Momma, I'm truly *scared*. I have never been so scared in all my life!"

Mrs. Irene remains silent as she gives her daughter her undivided attention.

Marlene's voice begins to crack as she thinks about how deeply she loves and cares about her son. "I love my baby boy, but I can't keep going through what I'm going through. Momma, I can't seem to get through to him, no matter what I do. No matter how hard I try, I just can't seem to reach him."

"Dear, I know. Believe me, I know. I know that you're trying your best to—"

"But nothing seems to be good enough for him. Momma, I'm losing my son, and it *hurts*. It hurts me so bad!" Marlene begins to weep as she reflects on the thought of losing her son.

"Now, now; don't cry. It's going to be okay. It's going to be all right. Please, dear, don't cry. We're going to get through this."

Marlene fights back the tears. "I just don't know what to do. Momma, do you think he'll listen to you? Could you see if he would be willing to listen to you? I know he used to love visiting with you, and he has always admired and respected you."

"Why, of course. I would love to talk with him," Mrs. Irene confidently states. She is deeply committed to helping her daughter and grandson to get things back on the right track.

Marlene begins to feel encouraged as she recalls the good times she, her mother, and Jamaal used to have when he was younger. She begins to reminiscence. "Momma, do you remember the times when we would attend his award ceremonies together, and the big smile that would come across his face when he noticed you in the audience?" Marlene begins to smile while gently wiping the tears from her eyes as she fondly thinks about the happy times spent with Jamaal and her mother.

Mrs. Irene also begins to smile as she reflects on the good old days. "Yes, I sure do remember. Those were precious moments, memories that I will cherish for the rest of my life."

"Momma, I want my baby boy back!" Marlene cries out in anguish.

"Yes, dear, I know. Trust me when I say that we're going to get our baby boy back. I'm willing to do whatever it takes to help you and Jamaal get things back on track. You know I love you, and it hurts me to see you going through the pain that you're going through right now. I have not seen you in this much pain since the divorce."

"Yeah, Ma, I know."

"You went through enough when you and Jamaal's father got divorced. Lord knows I love you and that baby boy of yours, and I'm not going to let the pain that the two of you are feeling get the best of you." Mrs. Irene slowly shakes her head from side to side as she thinks about what Jamaal must be going through. "You know that boy is hurting too. He's hurting just as badly as you are, but he's not able to talk about his pain, so he acts it out."

"You are so right, but I never imagined that the divorce would have this kind of effect on me or him. Jamaal didn't start acting out until he turned eight." Marlene pauses as she thinks about Jamaal's relationship with his father. "Wow! Do you know that that's around the time that his father completely stopped calling? He also stopped sending cards and giving him gifts for his birthday and on special occasions. Now that I think about it, his father has not given him a birthday gift since he was six years old."

"Baby, I know. That boy really *loved* his dad. That was all he would ever talk about when he came to visit. What he and his dad were going to do when his dad came to get him. I can't understand why his father stopped calling and visiting. It seems as though he vanished into thin air, without leaving a trace. Nobody has heard from him in quite some time."

Marlene begins to feel more and more resentful toward Jamaal's father for failing to keep in touch with them. Silence fills the air as she holds the phone to her ear.

Mrs. Irene can sense that talking about Jamaal's father is a sensitive topic for her daughter. She wittily shifts the conversation back to Jamaal. "Okay. So, when would be a good time for me to call to talk to Jamaal?"

Marlene excitedly replies, "Oh, Momma, I can ask him to stop by your house tomorrow after school."

"Sure, that would be great! I can get him to walk up to the corner store with me to do a little grocery shopping." Mrs. Irene smiles as she fondly thinks about spending time with her grandson.

"Easy on the sweets," Marlene lightheartedly advises. "You know that boy will have your grocery cart filled with nothing but candy, cake, cookies, ice cream, and chips—and leave me with a whopping dental bill to pay."

"Yeah, he's a lot like his mother," Mrs. Irene replies as she chuckles under her breath.

Marlene is deeply moved by her mother's love and support as tears form in the wells of her eyes. "Momma, I thank you. It is so good to smile again. I have not smiled since God knows when. Thank you for making me feel so much better. I don't know what I would do without you. I love you, Momma!"

"I love you too. You know I do." Mrs. Irene pauses as she thinks about inviting Marlene over for dessert. "I tell you what, maybe I can make my famous peach cobbler for dessert," she suggests. "I know how much you both love my peach cobbler with homemade vanilla ice cream on top."

"Yes, without a doubt. You do make the best peach cobbler in the whole wide world. Maybe I can come over and join the two of you for dessert."

"That sounds like a great idea! Now, you get some rest and try not to worry yourself sick. Worrying is not going to make it better. The good Lord above and Grandma will take care of that little man of yours. It really saddens me to see the two of you going through these changes, because he is such a fine young fellow, and God knows you have been a good mother *and* father to that precious child of yours."

Marlene fights back the tears. "Yeah, Ma, I really did not wish to involve you, but it seems like something is missing. I don't know where I went wrong. I have been trying to figure out what I did to cause Jamaal to turn on me the way that he has. I just can't figure it out."

"Baby girl, you have done the best you could, and it's not your fault. Stop blaming yourself. We will continue to pray and trust that God will reveal the answers to us in due time. Now, you get some rest, and I will see you tomorrow evening."

Marlene smiles as she thinks about how much she loves and appreciates her mother. "Yes, you sure will. Thanks, Ma. I love you."

"Me too, baby, me too." Mrs. Irene smiles as she reflects on how proud she is of her daughter.

Marlene is feeling very hopeful as she prepares to hang up the phone. "Good night, Momma."

"Good night, dear." After placing the telephone on the hook, Mrs. Irene kneels down to pray: "Lord, I pray that you will continue to watch over my daughter and her son. We do not know what is causing him to act out in the way that he does, but it is our prayer that you will reveal to us what is causing his anger. I love my daughter and my grandson, and I pray that you will give me the strength to help them get their relationship back on track. I am planning to meet with my grandson tomorrow after school, and I pray that he will be able to talk with me about all that is on his mind. Lord, I know that you are aware of all that Jamaal and his mother are going through. You also know the desires of my heart, and I pray that you will help Jamaal and his mother find peace and strength in knowing you. I thank you, Lord, for all that you have done, are doing, and plan to do in the life of my daughter and grandson. In Jesus's holy and righteous name I pray. Amen."

CHAPTER 3

THROUGH THE EYES OF A CHILD

Jamaal wakes up in a good mood. He thinks about how much fun he is going to have spending the day with Trevon and his crew. He becomes increasing hyped from listening to his favorite hip-hop station. However, he is still highly annoyed with his mother, and he is hoping to avoid coming in contact with her at all cost. Jamaal rushes to get dressed so that he can be on time to meet with Trevon and his crew.

Marlene, on the other hand, is in the kitchen preparing break-fast. She was able to get a good night's rest after talking with her mother about the challenges that she and Jamaal are going through. Marlene is in a good mood, and she feels optimistic about her relationship with her son, whom she loves dearly. She also is very excited about having Jamaal spend time with his grandmother, something that he has not done in quite some time. Marlene is hoping that Jamaal will take the time to eat, so that she can talk with him about visiting her.

Marlene hears Jamaal thumping down the stairs. She imme-diately calls out from the kitchen. "Jama-a-a-a-a-al!"

Jamaal continues to make his way down the stairs, still at-tempting to avoid coming in contact with his mother.

On hearing Jamaal racing down the hallway, Marlene

rushes over to the kitchen doorway and peers down the hall. "Jama-a-a-a-a-al! Jamaal, sweetheart, breakfast is ready!" she calls out. Marlene is desperately hoping that Jamaal will take the time to eat breakfast, and she continues to call him.

Jamaal is excited about meeting with Trevon and figures that he'd better respond, to avoid having to hear his mother's lecture about not responding when she calls him. Jamaal is wishing that she would just leave him alone, as he exasperatedly cries out, "Yeah—what?"

Marlene swiftly walks down the hallway toward Jamaal. She attempts to address his disrespectful tone by calmly calling out in a loving, yet firm, tone of voice, "Excuse me? I think you meant, 'Yes, ma'am.'"

Jamaal becomes increasingly irritated as he attempts to avoid coming in direct contact with his mother. He dashes into the den to grab his jacket. He shakes his head from side to side, while ignoring his mother's remark.

Marlene chooses not to dwell on Jamaal's highly irritable mood and rude behavior as she follows him into the den. "Jamaal, sweetheart, your grandmother asked if you would stop by after school. She would like to see you," Marlene informs him as she follows behind him, attempting to get his attention.

Jamaal does not respond as he slings his backpack across his shoulder.

"Jamaal, sweetheart, you have not spent time with your grandmother in quite some time, and she is looking forward to seeing you," Marlene tells him, while continuing to follow him from room to room.

Jamaal is highly annoyed by his mother's attempts at getting his attention. He grabs his headphones off the coffee table and does an about-face. He briskly walks past his mother while avoiding eye contact.

Marlene continues to follow Jamaal in hopes that he will respond. "Jamaal, your grandmother wants you to stop by after school this afternoon. She said that she also needs your help."

Jamaal shakes his head from side to side, lets out an exasperated sigh, and mumbles under his breath, "Yeah, whatever."

Marlene hears his smart remark. "Excuse me?" she replies.

Jamaal angrily snaps at his mother, "I said yeah! All right, I'll go! I'll stop by Grandma's house after school. Now, would you please leave me alone!"

Marlene is pleased that Jamaal has actually heard what she was saying. She manages to remain calm as she attempts to get Jamaal to eat breakfast. "Jamaal, breakfast is ready. Will you please take the time to eat before leaving the house?"

Jamaal is becoming highly annoyed by his mother following him around. *Man, I can't wait to get the heck out of this house! When I turn eighteen, I will be packing my bags and rolling up out of here. When I leave, I will not be coming back! I will never have to see this house again for as long as I live!* is what he is thinking as he heads toward the front door.

Marlene continues to follow Jamaal, making one final attempt to get him to eat before leaving the house. "Jamaal sweetheart, are you going to eat? Aren't you going to eat breakfast, son?" she passionately asks, continuing to overlook his rude behavior.

Jamaal grabs his keys off the mahogany nightstand next to the fireplace, turns to his mother, and brashly states, "No, I have to go! Can't you see I'm running late?" He races out of the house and slams the door, tugging at his jeans to keep them from falling to the ground.

Marlene assumes that Jamaal will be going straight to school. She is very excited about the thought of Jamaal spending time with his grandmother after school. She peers out the window at Jamaal as he jogs down the street. She smiles inwardly while thinking to herself, *That's my baby boy*. She calls Jamaal's grand-mother to let her know that he agreed to stop by after school.

Jamaal, on the other hand, is very excited about seeing Trevon as he jogs to the block where they agreed to meet. His excitement heightens as he thinks about skipping school to hang out with Trevon and his running partners. He begins to melodically hum and sing to himself while keeping an eye out for Trevon. "Baby, baby, baby. Man, I feel so free. It's so good to be out of that house. Man, my mother was starting to get on my *last nerve*! I can't wait to hook up with my man Tre and his crew. We're going to have us a good time."

Trevon notices Jamaal from a distance and calls out, "Hey, Jamaal! Over here!"

"Hey, man! What's up?" Jamaal asks as he jogs toward Trevon. "It is so good to see you," Jamaal tells him enthusiastically. "Man, I could not wait to get out the house this morning. Mom is still riding my back. I tell you, Tre, I could not *wait* to hook up with you and the crew!"

"Yeah, ditto." Trevon gives Jamaal a brotherly handshake as they walk over to Trevon's running partners. Trevon turns to Jamaal and begins to introduce him to the crew. "Let me intro-duce you to my boys," he says. "I have told them all about you. Now, this is my main man, Donte, but he goes by Black. This is Rasheed, better known as Slick. And this is Christopher. We call him Buster. My brother over here is Michael. He goes by Slapstick. Everybody calls me Maverick. And we decided that we would call you Tigger."

Jamaal smiles as he rocks from side to side. "Hey, I like that. Tigger! Yeah, I can get used to that."

"Hey, Jamaal, look here," Trevon calmly states. "Before we get started, we have to go over a few things, okay?" He is firmly looking Jamaal right in the eyes.

Jamaal shrugs his shoulders and nonchalantly agrees. "Okay."

"Look here, I need to be *sure* that you're down," Trevon insists while continuing to look Jamaal squarely in the eyes.

Jamaal is not sure of what Trevon is referring to, but he confidently replies, "No doubt; you know I'm down!"

"Okay, I thought so. But I just needed to be absolutely sure."

Jamaal keeps a straight face as he awaits further instruction from Trevon.

Trevon begins to share the rules that must be strictly adhered to in being a part of the crew: "Okay, first things first. I need to let you know that there is a code of secrecy that must not be broken under any circumstance. You gain access to the code after you complete the initiation process. You must be initiated before gaining entry into the brotherhood, and you never reveal a brother's real name nor rat anyone out under any circumstances. No matter what may be going on or happening around you, you have to maintain the code of secrecy. You got it?"

Jamaal is not sure of what the initiation process will entail. However, he is excited about being a part of Trevon's crew. "Yeah, I got it."

"Go-o-o-od! That's what I like to hear."

Jamaal really takes to Trevon and his friends, and they truly seem to like Jamaal. Jamaal feels understood, loved, supported, and accepted by the members of the gang, though he has not yet completed the initiation process. Feeling understood, loved, supported and accepted is something that Jamaal has not felt in quite some time, given the ongoing conflict with his mother.

As Jamaal goes through the initiation process, he is given a weapon. He is told that he must keep it with him at all times and that he may be forced to use it. Jamaal had no idea that he would be required to carry a weapon and expected to use and sell drugs, and the thought of backing out crosses his mind. This is more than he bargained for; however, he respects Trevon and wants to be there for him, even if it means risking his own life. Jamaal has never seen nor used drugs of any sort, and he is not sure what all this means.

They started the day by smoking marijuana, and later he is introduced to PCP and ecstasy. Jamaal notices that Trevon does not smoke the marijuana, nor does he use any of the other drugs, for that matter. Jamaal does not know what to make of Trevon's decision to abstain from using drugs. Jamaal is okay with trying the marijuana but is reluctant to try the PCP or ecstasy, because he does not know how they will affect him. Though he does not feel comfortable smoking the marijuana, he knows that he has to participate to be accepted into the gang. So he decides to try the marijuana but stays away from the other drugs.

As the day progresses, Jamaal begins to question his decision to join Trevon and his crew. He also begins to think about the promise he made to his mother to visit his grandmother after school. He knew that he would not be going to school when he left home earlier that morning. Jamaal deeply loves and respects his grandmother and has never wanted to let her down or disappoint her in any way. As he thinks about his love for his grandmother, different thoughts begin to race through his mind.

Trevon can tell that Jamaal is preoccupied and takes him aside to ask what is on his mind. Trevon respects Jamaal; he has always treated him like a younger brother. He also feels responsible for Jamaal but does not quite know why. There is just something special about Jamaal. Trevon also knows that Jamaal is different from the other members of the crew. As a result, he wants to make sure that Jamaal is absolutely sure of his decision before he gets too deeply involved in the initiation process and isn't able to back out. There is a special bond between Trevon and Jamaal. They seem to have an unspoken understanding about each other that makes it easy for Jamaal to be honest with Trevon about his feelings. Jamaal tells Trevon that he does not feel comfortable carrying a weapon. He also informs him that he did not know that he would be encouraged to use and sell drugs. Trevon respects Jamaal's decision and exempts him from any further involvement with the gang. Jamaal and Trevon agree to meet at seven thirty the following morning to talk further about what has happened.

Jamaal is relieved that he does not have to carry a weapon nor use or sell drugs. He respects Trevon all the more for exempting him from any further involvement with his crew. However, he is deeply concerned about Trevon. He fears that he will end up losing his life if he continues to buy and sell drugs. This experience causes Jamaal to think seriously about his life, and he tries to figure out his feelings toward his mother. He spends the balance of the afternoon sitting in the park, thinking about his life and how he has been treating his mother. He feels sad and disappointed in himself when he thinks about how his mother refuses to give up on him, no matter how he acts or what he does.

Jamaal looks down at his watch and is surprised at how fast the time has gone by. "Three thirty already!" Time to head to Grandma's house, he decides. As he is walking toward his grandmother's house, he thinks about the love and support that his mother and grandmother have shown him throughout his life, especially during the times in his life when nothing seemed to be going right.

As Jamaal approaches his grandmother's house, he attempts to fight back the tears. He stops to compose himself before walking up the steps onto the front porch. He takes a deep breath as he prepares to ring the doorbell.

Jamaal's grandmother has been anxiously awaiting his arrival, and she opens the door abruptly.

Jamaal is startled—he didn't expect his grandmother to be

waiting at the door. He leans into her outstretched arms and breathes a sigh of relief in knowing how much she truly cares. With a broad smile on his face, Jamaal utters, "Grandma, you startled me!"

Mrs. Irene reaches out to embrace Jamaal, and the smile on her face broadens.

Jamaal is comforted by his grandmother's warm embrace, and he tightly hugs her back, not wanting to let go.

Jamaal's grandmother can tell that he is in need of a hug, and she squeezes him tightly around his waist. "Now, that sure was a big hug! I tell you, it felt very special," she tells him affectionately. "How's my favorite grandson? I've missed seeing you."

Jamaal slowly releases his grip. He looks up at his grandmother and lovingly states, "Grandma, I've missed seeing you too." He then hesitates while looking her gently in the eyes. "But Grandma, there's something I need to tell you." He turns his head to the side and looks down at the floor, wondering how he will tell his grandma about what happened, without causing her to get upset or be disappointed in him.

Mrs. Irene can tell that there is something on Jamaal's mind. "Yes, dear, what is it?" she asks empathetically.

Jamaal desperately needs to talk with someone about what he has been through, and his grandmother is the only person whom he feels comfortable talking with, besides Trevon. Tears begin to fill his eyes as he looks up at her and softly whispers, "Grandma, I love you."

"I love you too, sweetheart." She extends her hand to him. "But what's the matter? Oh, come here. Come on over here, and have a seat next to Grandma. You know Grandma loves you. How have you been? What's been going on?"

Jamaal has no idea that his mother has informed his grandmother of the challenges that they have been going through.

He knows he needs someone to talk to as he hesitantly states, "Grandma, so much has been going on. I really don't know where to start."

"Now, now," Mrs. Irene states as she reaches over to give him a hug and rock him back and forth in her arms. "It's going to be all right. You're here with me, and you know I love you."

"Yeah, I know, but I feel so bad."

"It's going to be okay. You're here with Grandma. Trust me. Everything is going to be okay. You can talk to Grandma." Mrs. Irene continues to rock Jamaal in her arms.

Jamaal begins to feel better as he shares his feelings with his grandmother. "Yeah, I know. I know, Grandma, but I feel that I've let you down. I feel like I've let everybody down. I stopped visiting you and spending time with you. I'm failing all of my classes, and I haven't been going to school."

Mrs. Irene is surprised by what she is hearing, but she tries not to let it show. She remains calm, yet concerned, as she seeks clarification. "Excuse me. Did you say that you're failing all of your classes and have not been going to school?"

Jamaal humbly replies, "Yes, ma'am." Silence fills the air as Jamaal looks at his grandmother. He wonders how she is going to respond.

Though shocked by what she is hearing, Mrs. Irene calmly states, "Go on. I'm listening." She encourages Jamaal to continue to share as she gives him her undivided attention.

"No, ma'am, I haven't been going to school," Jamaal shyly admits. "I cut school today so that I could hang out with a friend of mine named Trevon. He's the only person that I feel understands me, and we seem to have a special friendship that's hard to explain. There's something special about Trevon, and I'm not quite sure what it is."

"Hmm, tell me more about your friend Trevon."

"Well, he's fifteen years old and is repeating the eighth grade for the second time. He does not go to class, and he is not what you and Momma would consider the best role model." Jamaal pauses as he wonders how much he should share. "But Grandma, he is very smart and seems to care about people."

Mrs. Irene remains silent while giving Jamaal her undivided attention.

Jamaal pauses as he thinks about the day he and Trevon first met. He decides to share his experience with his grandmother. "Grandma, Trevon and I met at school. We met in the boys' bathroom. I got *so mad* in class one afternoon, and I asked to be excused from class because I felt like I was going to lose it." Jamaal becomes tearful as he recalls the day that he and Trevon first met.

"Now, now. It's okay, baby. I'm listening."

Jamaal can no longer fight back the tears. He begins to weep as he continues to share how he and Trevon first met. "Grandma, when I went in the bathroom, I was so angry that I just began to cry. It was almost as though I could not control myself. I just burst out crying."

"Sweetheart, it is okay," states Mrs. Irene. She grabs a Kleenex and gently wipes the tears from Jamaal's eyes. "It's going to be okay."

Jamaal regains his composure as he continues to recount his experience. "I had been thinking about my father and the fights that Mom and I have been getting into at home, and I was beginning to feel like no one cared about me. The teachers were getting on my case, and I was starting to feel like I couldn't do *anything* right."

"It's going to be okay," Mrs. Irene reassures him. She places her arm around Jamaal's shoulder and lovingly pulls him to her side.

"Grandma, I thought that I was the only one in the bathroom. Then, after boiling my eyes out crying, I looked up and saw

Trevon. He was leaning up against one of the sinks. As I looked up at him, he assured me that it was all right and that things would get better. It was as though he understood why I was crying, without my having to tell him anything about myself or about my life. Grandma, he didn't make fun of me or make me feel bad for crying. He just encouraged me and made me believe in my heart that things would get better."

Mrs. Irene discreetly wipes the tears from her own eyes as she listens intently to her grandson's story about how he and Trevon first met. "Trevon sounds like a very special person," she confidently asserts.

"Yeah, Grandma, he *really* is," Jamaal agrees with a slight smile. He is beginning to feel better. "Grandma, there's so much that I need to tell you about what's been going on, but I don't know where to start."

"You're doing a great job, sweetheart. You just take your time. Grandma is not going anywhere anytime soon. This is our special time together, and we have all evening. You can even spend the night if you'd like." Jamaal's grandmother looks him in the eyes as she smiles. She is thinking about how nice it would be to have Jamaal spend the night.

"Oh, Grandma. I would love to spend the night with you," Jamaal says with a smile.

"Okay then!" Mrs. Irene excitedly concludes. "We can plan for you to spend the night, because I need to spend some *quality time* with my grandson. I'll call your mom and let her know you are here with me and make sure it's okay for me to keep you until it's time for you to go to school tomorrow. You are planning to go to school tomorrow, right?" she asks with a raised eyebrow as she leans her head to the side while awaiting Jamaal's response.

Jamaal smiles broadly as he enthusiastically exclaims, "Yes, ma'am!"

"That's my boy! Everything is going to be all right." Jamaal's grandmother kisses him on the top of his head as she prepares to call his mother to let her know that all is well and that Jamaal will be spending the night with her.

Marlene joyfully agrees to her mother's plan. She begins to feel more and more hopeful that she and Jamaal will be able to get things back on track.

Jamaal looks on as his grandmother talks on the phone with his mother.

Mrs. Irene turns to Jamaal and asks, "Okay now, where were we?" as she prepares to hang up the phone.

"I was telling you about my friend Trevon," he says excitedly.

"Oh yeah, that's right. And I was saying that he seems like a very special friend."

"Yeah, he's a *great* friend. He's about the only person who understands me. Trevon really seems to understand what I've been going through."

"Yes, sweetheart, and I'm very interested in hearing more about what you've been going through."

"Well, to tell you the truth, Grandma, it's me and Mom. We just can't seem to get along, and she seems to be *sad* all the time. She's always crying, and if she's not crying, we're getting into it. We're always fussing and fighting, and things reached a point where I didn't think anyone cared about me. My teachers were even talking about placing me in a special school, and Grandma, Mom didn't seem to care. Dad stopped caring a long time ago, and it didn't even seem like my teachers cared anymore. Grandma, I got to the point where *I* stopped caring. Nothing or nobody mattered to me anymore."

"Oh, my," gasps Mrs. Irene as she attempts to comfort her grandson. "You really have been through a lot."

"Grandma, to be honest, I never felt like my dad cared about me. If he did, he wouldn't treat me like he does. It just doesn't seem like anyone cares, and I don't have anyone to talk to about my feelings. Nobody listens! The only person that I feel cares about me is Trevon. He's the only person that I feel I can talk to without feeling judged or criticized."

"Yeah, I know, baby. I understand." Jamaal's grandmother continues to support and encourage him as he expresses his innermost thoughts and feelings.

"Grandma, I miss spending time with you, but I really miss my dad. I can't understand why he doesn't love and care about me anymore. Grandma, what did I do to make my daddy stop loving me?"

"Now, my dear child. Please *hear me* when I say that your father loves you. And, *trust me* when I say that you could never do anything to cause anyone to stop loving you. Love is unconditional, and if a person truly loves you, there is nothing that you could ever do to cause that person to stop loving you." Mrs. Irene pauses to make sure Jamaal fully understands what she is saying, and she gives him a moment to process what has been said.

Jamaal remains silent while continuing to give his grandmother his undivided attention.

"Baby, adults may not always agree with the things that you do, but that does not mean that they do not love you. We are here to help you to become the best person that you can possibly be. And in becoming the best person that you can possibly be, you will have to make some tough choices."

Mrs. Irene's genuine love for Jamaal makes it easy for him to tell her about what happened earlier in the day with Trevon and his crew. "Yeah, I know. You mean like the choice that I had to make today when I was with Trevon and his friends?"

Jamaal's grandmother has no idea what Jamaal is referring to, and she is surprised by his comment. However, she doesn't allow her emotions to show as she replies, "Yes, like the choice you had to make today when you were with Trevon and his friends."

"Grandma, it was a difficult choice, and I took a chance on losing Trevon as my friend."

Mrs. Irene appreciates Jamaal's openness as she continues to give him her undivided attention. "Yes, I'm sure. How do you feel about the choice that you made?" she asks.

"It was a tough decision, but I know that I made the right choice. I could not do what they were asking me to do, but I clearly understood why they made the choices that they made. Trevon does not talk about his family that much, but he once told me about how he would come home to find his mother high on drugs, and how his baby sister would be crying because she had not been fed or taken care of." Jamaal pauses as he thinks about Trevon's plight. He empathizes with his friend Trevon, as he passionately recalls: "Trevon said that he often struggled to fight back the tears while attempting to remain strong for his family. Not only that, he said that his younger brothers would be sitting on the couch in front of the television with a look of sadness in their eyes. It was like they were waiting on him to come home to take care of them." Jamaal's eyes begin to fill with tears as he cries out, "Grandma, Trevon has really had a hard life. His mother has been addicted to crack cocaine for as long as he can remember, and he has never seen or known his father."

Mrs. Irene gingerly wipes the tears from Jamaal's eyes. "Wow, your friend Trevon truly does have a lot going on."

"Yes, ma'am," Jamaal sheepishly agrees as he looks up at his grandmother. "When Trevon introduced me to his running partners and talked about initiating me into their group, I was very excited. I was looking forward to being a part of the crew. But when they told me I would have to carry a weapon and might have to use it, I began to think about you and Mom. I know that I have hurt Mom in a lot of ways, but it was hard for me to put my life at risk knowing what it would do to the family."

Mrs. Irene is shocked by what she is hearing but does not let it show. She reaches over and gives Jamaal a hug. She then looks him in the eyes and firmly states, "Baby, you made the right choice, and I'm *very proud* of you!"

"Grandma, you don't know how good that makes me feel." Jamaal inwardly smiles as he thinks about how much his grandmother loves and cares about him. "Thank you for being there for me."

"You're quite welcome, baby."

"Grandma, you know that I have never meant to hurt you or Momma, and I want to apologize to you both," Jamaal sincerely states as he looks into his grandmother's eyes. "It's just that I have so many different feelings going on inside of me at one time, and they make me so sad, mad, and angry. I was once so upset that I felt I could literally hurt anybody that got in my way. It was as if I was mad at the world. I don't like feeling that way, but it seemed like I just couldn't help it. Sometimes I've wished that I hadn't been born."

Mrs. Irene hugs Jamaal tightly and warmly declares, "Now, now. I don't want you to be thinking like that. You're my baby boy, and I'm so glad that you were born."

Jamaal can literally feel the warmth of his grandmother's embrace as he closes his eyes. She tightly embraces him, and he tenderly hugs her back.

Jamaal's grandmother slowly releases her embrace while looking him squarely in the eyes, as she compassionately asserts, "Your mother knows that you never meant to hurt her, and I know that she loves you *very, very much*. I also know that she has never meant to hurt you, even though there have been times when you have felt very hurt by your mother."

"Grandma, I know that you love me, and I know deep down in my heart that Mom loves me too. But sometimes, I just don't *feel* like Momma loves me. Sometimes I don't feel like anybody loves me."

Mrs. Irene places her arm around Jamaal's shoulder, as he continues to reveal his feelings.

"Grandma, I sometimes feel the same way about Momma as I do about Dad. Mom and I used to do fun things together, like going to the amusement park, and she used to buy me things all the time. She would buy me anything I wanted, and I really miss the times when she used to read me a bedtime story and tuck me in for the night. It seems like everything just *stopped* all of a sudden. Almost the same way Daddy stopped doing all the fun things he used to do, like calling, visiting, and sending me birthday cards and gifts. They both just stopped caring about me. It almost seemed like *no one* cared about me anymore."

"Oh, sweetheart. I bet your mother never realized how much those special activities meant to you. You have done such a wonderful job talking with me. Would you be willing to talk with your mother about how you feel?"

"Grandma, Momma doesn't listen to me. All she does is nag! We *never* talk. It's like she doesn't have time for me anymore."

Fully understanding his mood and his sentiments toward his mother, Jamaal's grandmother smiles as she replies, "Oh, I'm sure that's not the case. I bet if you asked your mom, she would gladly make time for you."

Jamaal shakes his head from side to side in disbelief. "I don't know, Grandma. I'm afraid to ask, because I don't know what she's going to say."

"Well, we will never know unless we ask. We can call her right now, if you'd like."

"You ask her, Grandma. I'm afraid she might say 'no.'"

"Sure. I will gladly ask her for you."

Jamaal is somewhat nervous, and he remains silent. He remains silent with his eyes fixed on his grandmother as she picks up the phone and dials his mother's number.

Marlene cheerfully answers. "Hello!"

"Hello, dear."

"Hi, Ma. How's it going?"

"Better than you could ever imagine!"

"Oh, that's wonderful!"

"Yes, it is, and Marlene, your son has something very important to share with you."

"Really? What is it? Is he okay?"

"Yes, dear; he's fine. And he's definitely a child you should be very proud of."

"Yes, I know! You know that I am. Momma, I love my baby boy, but I just don't know what has gotten into him."

"Yes dear, *I* know, but I don't think *he knows* how much you love him. I also think that you and your son need to spend some quality time together. Believe it or not, he misses you about as much as he misses his dad."

Jamaal leans his head to the side and listens intently as his grandmother converses with his mother.

"Momma, what do you mean?" Marlene is confused by what she is hearing and passionately cries out, "I've always been here! I haven't gone anywhere. His dad is the one who has not been around."

Mrs. Irene remains calm as she replies, "Yeah, baby, I know. But he misses you *and* his dad. I will explain what I mean later, but for now, your son *really needs* his mother. He doesn't feel like you have time for him anymore. He misses all the fun things the two of you used to do together, like going to the amusement park, special outings together, bedtime stories, and tucking him in at night."

Muriel Kennedy, PhD

Marlene is flooded with emotions, and she nearly drops the phone. She suddenly begins to realize how she has inadvertently neglected her son. "Oh my, I never knew those things meant so much to him!" she cries out. "With the promotion and increase in responsibilities in my current position, I have *totally* neglected my son without realizing it! That was something I said I would never do. Oh, Momma, could you please put Jamaal on the phone? I need to speak with him."

"Jamaal, sweetheart, your mother would like to speak with you." Jamaal's grandmother passes the telephone to him. Jamaal has been listening intently to the conversation between his grandmother and his mother. His voice begins to crack and tears begin to well up in his eyes, as he slowly raises the phone to his ear. "Hi, Mom."

Marlene, fighting back the tears, immediately replies with deep conviction. "Oh, my dear, please forgive me for neglecting you! I didn't know that you felt let down by my not spending time with you. My dear child, please accept my sincere apologies!" Marlene pauses as she takes a moment to compose herself while continuing to fight back the tears. "I'll tell you what. When you come home, we're going to have a special talk, just you and me. Then we will rent a movie, and we can have chili cheese dogs with coleslaw on top, Carolina style barbeque potato chips, and your favorite ice-cream soda to go along with it. How does that sound?"

Jamaal is surprised by his mother's reference to renting a movie. He hadn't thought that she was listening when he'd asked her several months ago to take him to Blockbusters to rent a movie. Jamaal wants to let his mother know about his friend Trevon, but he doesn't know how to go about sharing his experience. He pauses, thinking about how easy it was for him to share with his grandmother, and then he timidly states, "Mom."

44

"Yes, dear?" she asks. She is anxious to know what is on his mind.

Jamaal nervously asserts, "Mom, I have something that I need to tell you about my friend Trevon, and I hope you won't get mad or start to hate me again."

Marlene becomes tearful as the idea of her son thinking that she hates him races through her mind. "Jamaal, sweetheart, I can honestly say that I love you more than you could ever imagine. I may not always agree with what you do or say, but that does not mean that I hate you. You are my one and only child. I gave birth to you, and I could never, ever hate you. Do you understand?"

"Yes, ma'am. I understand."

"Sweetheart, you mean the world to me—and I hope you know that!"

Jamaal is surprised, and his face shows it. He has never heard his mother speak so fondly of him. "Momma, that's the same thing that Grandma said!"

"Yes, you mean the world to me *and* your grandmother, and we would not trade you for anything in this whole, wide world," Marlene fervently states. "Now, I'm going to let you spend the night with Grandma, but I want you to promise me that we will spend special time together tomorrow night." Her smile broadens as she continues, "And the next night, and the next night, and the next night, and the next night, and the next night—until there are no more nights left to spend with my baby boy."

Jamaal chuckles at his mother's remark. He is beginning to realize how much his mother truly does care about him. "Yes, ma'am, I promise." Jamaal turns to his grandmother as he prepares to give her the phone. But before handing it over, Jamaal pauses as he seeks to get his mother's attention. "Oh, Momma."

"Yes, dear?"

Jamaal pauses as he smiles while softly confiding, "I love you."

Jamaal's mother smiles and tears come to her eyes as she replies, "I love you too, son. I love you too."

Jamaal smiles as he passes the phone to his grandmother. "Here, Grandma."

Mrs. Irene is beaming as she takes the phone. "Marlene dear, I tell you, you have one fine young fellow, who truly is able to express himself when adults take the time to listen."

"Yeah, Ma, I know. I also have one very fine mother, whom I love more than you could ever imagine. Momma, but seriously, I want to thank you for everything. I can never repay you for all you have done for me and my son."

Mrs. Irene looks Jamaal in the eyes, as she lovingly states, "You have already repaid me, dear, by giving me this wonderful grandson of mine and by being the wonderful daughter that you have always been. Now I must go. I have an anxious little fellow here who can't wait until the night is over so that he can spend quality time with his mother. I have decided that we'll go out for dinner. We would invite you, but you know what they say: 'Two's company and three's a crowd.'" She then turns to Jamaal with a smile and a wink.

"Yes, I know," Marlene says, and she is smiling too. "You just want little Jamaal all to yourself. I can understand that." Marlene chuckles while lightheartedly stating, "I know what restaurant you guys will be going to, but I promise not to crash the party."

"Yes, you know me all too well. I may need to switch up my routine." Mrs. Irene chuckles as she leans down and gently kisses Jamaal on the forehead.

Marlene laughs as she prepares to hang up the phone. "Momma, please give my little one a kiss for me after you read him his bedtime story, pray, and tuck him in for the night." Marlene pauses as she adds, "I love you, Momma."

"Yes, I know. I love you too, and do have a good night." Mrs. Irene thinks about how blessed she is to have such a loving and caring daughter and grandson as she prepares to hang up the phone.

"Thanks, Ma. Good night." Marlene leans her head back on the couch as she prepares to hang up the phone at her end. She reflects on the conversation that she has just had with her mother and son.

Mrs. Irene places the phone on the hook and turns to Jamaal. "Okay now, where were we?"

Jamaal replies with great affection, giving his grandmother a tight hug and a kiss. "Grandma, thank you for listening to me and for always being there for me. You're the greatest!"

"Jamaal, sweetheart, I wouldn't have it any other way!"

Jamaal smiles with glee, and he is overjoyed by the love that his mother and grandmother both have for him.

"How would you like to go on a special outing with Grandma?"

"Oh, Grandma, I would love that!"

"Okay, let's go." Jamaal's grandmother grabs her purse and reaches for his arm. They lock elbows and head out the door.

Jamaal grins and holds his head high as he escorts his grandmother to the car. "How could I have *ever* questioned yours and Momma's love for me?" Jamaal asks as he thinks about spending quality time with his mother. "Grandma, I can't wait to talk with Mom. I'm also looking forward to seeing Trevon tomorrow morning—*before* school."

"Sweetheart, I'm sure that they will be looking forward to seeing and talking with you as well. Now, I want you to keep that beautiful smile and never let anyone or anything cause you to question my love or your mother's love for you ever again. You are our baby boy, and we will *always* be here for you."

"Thank you, Grandma. I needed to hear that. You make me

feel so special, and I thank you. I'm so glad that you're my grand-mother. I wish all of my friends had grandmothers like you."

"Oh, Jamaal baby, that's so sweet of you to say. Now, I want you to keep that charm of yours. Trust me, it will get you very far in life."

"Yes, ma'am," Jamaal replies, and he begins to blush.

Jamaal and his grandmother head to the family's favorite restaurant, to spend some more quality time talking and getting caught up on all that has been going on in Jamaal's life while enjoying a scrumptious three-course meal.

After returning to his grandmother's house, Jamaal calls his friend Trevon, to ask if they can meet at seven o'clock in the morning instead of seven thirty so that he will not be late for school.

Trevon happily agrees.

CHAPTER 4

THROUGH THICK AND THIN

Trevon wakes up in a solemn mood and slowly gets out of bed. Why can't he have a mother who would motivate him to achieve his dreams of owning his own business? Then he would be encouraged to stay in school and get his degree in hope of being successful in life. He begins to think about how, as a child, he had overheard members of his family speaking about his mother's drug addiction. In being the oldest, this caused him to feel that he had to step in and take care of his younger brothers and baby sister. The reality of not knowing his father and having a mother who seemed to care more about using drugs than taking care of her five children weighed heavily on Trevon; it was a lot for him to deal with on his own.

Trevon rushes to get dressed while thinking about how Jamaal has become a source of inspiration for him. He looks forward to seeing Jamaal and spending time with him. Trevon is excited about talking with Jamaal, as he walks to the spot where they are to meet. He thinks about how positive and upbeat Jamaal always is. His relationship with Jamaal has helped him remain committed to living another day.

Jamaal leaves his grandmother's house around the time that he would normally leave his mother's house in order to arrive on time to meet Trevon. He is excited about meeting with him. However, it takes him a little longer than he anticipated to get there. Jamaal looks down at his watch and realizes that he is going to be late. He begins to jog. He worries to himself that Trevon will think he stood him up.

Trevon, meanwhile, is puzzled by the fact that Jamaal has not arrived. *Wow! Jamaal is usually the one waiting for me*, he thinks to himself. He is perplexed, and his anxiety begins to show as a series of thoughts cross his mind: *I wonder what's keeping Jamaal. I wonder if he is going to show up. He's the one person who has not disappointed me or let me down. Man, I hope he shows up, because I really need someone to talk to.* Trevon breathes a sigh of relief as he looks up and notices Jamaal in the distance, jogging toward the park. Trevon begins to smile as he runs over to meet Jamaal. He whispers under his breath, "Wow! There he is—my one and only true friend. I knew that he wouldn't let me down."

Jamaal smiles as he notices Trevon jogging toward him. "Hey, Tre," he calls out. "What's up? How's it going?"

Trevon is excited to see Jamaal yet still somewhat despondent, but he tries not to let it show. "I'm good. But I'm really looking forward to talking with you." Trevon gives Jamaal a brotherly hug as he thinks about how much he respects and admires him.

Noticing Trevon's mood, Jamaal becomes concerned. "Hey, man, is everything okay? Your mom and siblings are okay, right?"

Trevon shrugs his shoulders. "Yeah, Mom's fine; nothing out of the ordinary. And yes, my siblings are okay, for the most part. We're getting by the best way we know how."

"Man, that's good to hear. I was starting to worry about you there for a minute. I don't know what I would do if anything happened to you, or anyone else in your family, for that matter."

Trevon gazes up at the sky as he reflects on how good it feels to have someone care so much about him and his family. "Jamaal, man, I don't know what I'd do without you. You are the first person who has cared anything about me since my grandmother died. And, man, I tell you what, life can really get you down if you let it."

"You got that right!" Jamaal pauses, reflecting on the fact that Trevon does not appear to be himself. "But Trevon, man, this is not like you. You're always so full of life," he states while looking Trevon in the eyes. "Man, every time I'm around you I feel like I'm on top of the world. Are you sure you're all right?"

"Nothing for you to worry about; nothing that I can't handle." Trevon shakes his head from side to side as he thinks about his life.

Jamaal is not convinced. He places his hand on Trevon's shoulder while asking, "Are you sure?" He attempts to reassure Trevon of his support, stating emphatically, "You know I'm here for you and always will be. Man, I've got your back. If there is anything you need to talk to me about, you know that I'm here for you."

"Yeah, I know," Trevon calmly replies. Thoughts are racing through his mind. He pauses as he thinks about Jamaal's comments, and he gains the courage to share some of what is on his mind. "Jamaal, man, it's cool you say that, because there is something that I need to talk with somebody about. Someone I can truly trust. And believe it or not, but you are the first person that I have felt that I could really trust since my grandmother passed away— that was over five years ago." Trevon chokes up as he looks Jamaal in the eyes and states, "But Jamaal, man, I don't want to burden you with my problems."

"Trevon, you know that you can talk to me. You were there for me, and the least you can do is allow me to be there for you," asserts Jamaal as he gently places his hand on Trevon's shoulder. "Look, we're blood. We're best friends, man, and the best of friends we'll be to the end."

"Yeah, I know."

Jamaal and Trevon spontaneously begin to walk toward the school grounds.

Trevon looks away from Jamaal as he fights back the tears. "I tell you, man, no one can begin to imagine how much freaking pressure I've been under. I don't think there has been a day when I've been able to go home and not have to worry about whether or not we were going to be busted in on by the cops or get kicked out of our house for failing to pay rent." Trevon feels himself getting upset. He shakes his head from side to side as feelings of disdain toward his mother begin to surface. "Jamaal, man, I don't need to go into that drama. You know my story," he angrily states. His tone is dismissive as he looks Jamaal in the eyes.

Jamaal is speechless as he solemnly shakes his head from side to side.

"Jamaal, you know how I told you a while back about my mother being addicted to drugs, and how I would come home to find my brothers and baby sister crying because they hadn't been fed?"

"Yeah, I remember."

"Well, when I was younger, I would often dream of having my own business and being able to take care of my mother and my brothers and our baby sister. Don't get me wrong, I do love my mother. She's all I got, but I can't stand the way she's wasting her life away. Man, it makes me so freaking *angry*!"

Jamaal remains silent.

"Man, you're not going to believe this, but I have the kind of anger in me that can really hurt a person if they rub me the wrong way. I hate it when I get like that, but there have been times when I have actually had thoughts of taking my anger out on other people when they say or do things that upset me or make me mad."

Jamaal looks Trevon in the eyes in disbelief, as he passionately responds, "But Trevon, man, you always seem so happy. I can't imagine you getting *that* mad or upset."

Trevon chuckles and replies, "Yeah, I may seem happy when I'm around you. But Jamaal, there is so much that you don't know about me and probably wouldn't understand."

"Yeah, that may be true, but why does life have to be so dog-gone complicated?"

"I really don't know," Trevon says with a sigh. He shrugs his shoulders and shakes his head from side to side. "But I tell you what, in seeing what drugs have done to my mother, *and* my family, I have made up my mind that I will not allow drugs to do the same thing to me. At the age of ten I vowed to never use drugs, for as long as I live. Jamaal, believe it or not, but my goal is to make something out of my life and to help my mother get off drugs so that she can be a mother to my younger brothers and our baby sister."

Jamaal empathizes with Trevon as he chimes in, "Man, I thought I had it bad. God only knows what my father is up to and the reason he chose to forget that he had a son. He acts like I don't exist. Trevon, man, parents can't even begin to imagine the pain that they cause their children, and I often wonder if they even care." Jamaal lets out a deep sigh. "To tell the truth, if I had known that my life would turn out like this, I would have preferred to have not been born."

Knowing he's not alone, Trevon begins to cheer up. He smiles and animatedly states, "Trust me, man; I know *exactly* what you mean." Jamaal and Trevon let out hearty laughs as they give each other a high five.

Trevon is anxious to continue sharing his life experience with Jamaal; he picks up where he left off. "Well, as I was saying, I vowed to abstain from drugs for as long as I lived. However, at the age of twelve, the opportunity to sell drugs was staring me straight in the face, and I said, 'What the heck.'"

Jamaal's eyes widen as Trevon makes reference to selling drugs at the age of twelve.

Trevon continues in a bold, yet lighthearted manner. "Man, you know me well enough to know that I've got *mad skills*. When this older dude approached me about selling drugs, I didn't have to think twice. I knew that I would be one of the best hustlers in the business and saw it as a way to keep a roof over my family's head," Trevon explains as he shrugs his shoulders in a nonchalant manner. "To be honest, it seemed like I had no other choice. We needed the money to survive. So, I took these guys up on their offer, and I have been dealing drugs ever since."

Jamaal is shocked by Trevon's confession. Incredulously he replies, "No way! You're telling me that you started selling drugs at the age of twelve? Trevon, man, you've *got* to be kidding me."

Jamaal's innocence is something that Trevon has admired while secretly wishing that he was more like Jamaal. He responds with a slight smile. "Nope. No joke. Hustling has become a way of life for me. I don't agree with what I'm doing, and I wish I could give it up. However, it makes me feel good to know that I can feed my brothers and sister, keep clothes on their backs, and have a roof over their heads."

Jamaal admires the pride and joy that Trevon seems to feel in being able to take care of his younger brothers and sister. He remains silent as he continues to give Trevon his undivided attention.

"I also feel good about the fact that I've been able to keep my family from getting evicted. We've received several eviction notices, and I thank God that we still have a roof over our heads."

"Yeah, man, that is good," agrees Jamaal. He'd had no idea that Trevon's life was as complicated as that! How had he managed to make it this far in life without giving up? Jamaal wonders.

As Trevon begins to think about his mother, thoughts of being deprived of his childhood begin to enter his mind, and feelings of anger and resentment begin to surface. "I'm sorry, Jamaal, but I'm getting fed up with my mother's *crap!* To tell you the truth, my mother doesn't have a clue of what she's been putting us through. It's almost as though she couldn't care less about what happens to all of us."

Jamaal continues to listen with a deep sense of sadness and genuine concern. He begins to feel helpless, but he refuses to give up as he tries to figure out how he can best help his friend during his time of greatest need.

"It doesn't seem like my mother cares about any of her kids, and that is what hurts the most. And, to be honest with you, there have been times when I could honestly not care less about what happens to me. Man, I couldn't care less about my life. My life means *nothing*. The people I'm most concerned about are my younger brothers and our baby sister. Jamaal, man, I would have given up on life a long time ago if not for them. They have forced me to hang on and hang in there, in spite of all that we've been going through."

"Okay! Okay! Man, I see. I understand. I *truly* do understand. But what I want to know is whether you're willing to give it up. Selling drugs is no way to live. You can end up getting *killed!*"

"I appreciate your concern, but I honestly can't say that I am willing to give it up."

"Come on, man, I'm sure we can figure this thing out. If you want to give it up, I can help. I can talk to my mom; I'm sure she knows people who can help us."

"I don't know, Jamaal. It's not that easy."

"What do you mean, not that easy? We can do this man—I *know* we can!" Jamaal exclaims with deep conviction.

"I'm not sure. Jamaal, man, I'm not sure if I'm ready," Trevon calmly replies as he shakes his head from side to side. "I don't know how my family will make it without the money. Man, I'm making big bucks. Don't get me wrong, I want my mother to get help and all, and I know I need help too. But Jamaal, man, I don't know what to do." Trevon pauses while looking Jamaal in the eyes as he emphatically asserts in a sarcastic tone, "Huh! I know graduating high school and going to college is *not* an option."

Jamaal remains serious and does not feed into Trevon's sarcasm as he firmly declares, "Man, we'll just have to take it one step at a time. We'll figure this thing out."

"Yeah, I tell you what—I had convinced myself that I couldn't care less about what happened to me ..." Trevon pauses as he thinks about the positive impact that Jamaal has had on his life. He continues to look him squarely in the eyes. "But knowing you has helped me to begin to appreciate life."

Jamaal remains silent as he intently listens to Trevon.

"Jamaal, man, I have been dealing drugs for the past three years, and I must say that I'm pretty good at it. I've been in shootouts and can truly say that I have witnessed my fair share of drug busts and arrests." Trevon pauses as he reflects on the close calls that could have resulted in his own death. "Now that I think about it, I'm amazed that I am still alive and have not had to take another person's life to save my own."

Jamaal is stunned as he listens to Trevon speak about shootouts. Trevon is the first person that Jamaal has ever known to deal drugs.

"In looking back, I now know that God has been watching over me and has kept me safe. If it had not been for God, man, I'm sure that I would have been dead a long time ago."

"Yes, I thank God that you are still alive! Trevon, I don't agree with what you're doing, but I want you to know that I'm here for you and always will be, no matter what. You know I've got your back... right?"

Trevon smiles as he jokingly says, "Tigger, man, I tell you. I don't know what I'm going to do with you. You're pretty *tough*." Trevon pauses as his mood shifts. "But on a serious note, I do thank you for hearing me out and continuing to be there for me."

Jamaal smiles as he boldly expresses, "Trevon, you'd better believe me when I say I'm not going to let anything happen to you. I couldn't live with the thought of you not being around." Jamaal gives Trevon a brotherly hug as they both fight back the tears.

Warmed by Jamaal's friendship, Trevon stares hard at him to ensure that he has his undivided attention, and then he firmly asserts, "Now, hear me when I say we're going to get your little smart butt back in school. And from this day forward, you're going to attend *all* of your classes and get yourself back on the honor roll, or else you will have to answer to me."

"Yes, sir," Jamaal crisply retorts with a smile as he playfully salutes Trevon. He snaps his hand down to his side while bluntly stating, "And now, I want to share a serious note with you." This time Jamaal stares Trevon down as he firmly states, "I want you to give me permission to talk with my mother about our friendship and all that you are dealing with. Maybe she can help you and your family get the help you all need."

Trevon thinks about how he does not wish to burden Jamaal and his mother with his family's drama. He shakes his head from side to side. He stares at the ground while hesitantly stating, "I don't know, Jamaal. Man, can we just let it go? Why waste your time?" Trevon lets out a big sigh as he looks up at the sky. He then turns to Jamaal and says gratefully, "Jamaal, to be quite honest, I do appreciate your being a true friend in taking the time to hear me out. But as we both know, there are no easy answers to my family drama. Jamaal, man, my family's got issues on top of issues. There's absolutely *no hope* for my family."

"Yeah, man, I know exactly what you mean, and I know that

there are no easy answers." Jamaal can understand where Trevon is coming from, and he wants Trevon to *know* that he understands. "Look at my life," he emphatically states. "You know better than anybody else what I've been through with *my* mother."

Trevon remains silent as he begins to mentally compare his life to Jamaal's.

Jamaal thinks about all that he and his mother have been through over the past couple of months and how she has refused to give up on him. "No doubt my mother can be a royal pain at times," he reflects, "as I'm sure you know. But believe it or not, she also can be a good listener." Jamaal places his hand on Trevon's shoulder and confidently states, "Trevon, I want you to know that you can trust my mother in the same way you trust me. My mother and my grandmother are the only people in my life who have never failed me. To tell the truth, they should have given up on me a long time ago, but they didn't. Now that I think about it, they are the ones who taught me how to love and trust people, and I know without a shadow of a doubt that my mother can help you and your family."

Trevon has a high level of respect for Jamaal's mother and grandmother, and he begins to smile as he senses the genuine love and concern that Jamaal has for him. He chuckles to himself as he gives in to Jamaal's plea. "Okay, I'm definitely feeling you. If you think it will help, I'm willing to go along with it. I trust you, and it can't hurt, but until I'm able to figure this thing out, you know what I will be up to."

"No! Until *we* are able to figure this thing out, you know what *we* will be up to. Now, I want you to check in with me *daily* to let me know that you're okay. I don't care if it's two o'clock in the morning; I want you to *call me!*" Jamaal makes sure he has Trevon's attention as he seeks his acknowledgment. "You got that?" Without hesitating, Jamaal declares, "If I don't hear from you, I'm going to come looking for you, and that's a promise."

Trevon chuckles as he jokingly states, "I know that you're my boy and all, but you're starting to sound more and more like a father."

Jamaal remains serious as he brushes Trevon's comment off. "Yeah, whatever," he retorts. "Who knows what our fathers would be saying *if* they were around."

"Yeah, *if*—and that's a big if—they were around," Trevon interjects. He thinks about the father he has never met. "Who knows where they are or what they're up to," Trevon snaps. "For all we know, they could have other kids out there that they are not willing to take care of."

"Yeah, as the saying goes, 'It's easy to be a daddy, but it takes a real man to be a father,'" Jamaal sarcastically exclaims. "Man, later for them! I tell you what, we've got each other, and that's better than any *deadbeat* father, as far as I'm concerned."

"I know that's right!" Trevon raises his hand and gives Jamaal a high five.

Jamaal smiles as he slaps hands with Trevon. He then says firmly, "Now, I want you to know that I will be at school and in class under one condition ..." Jamaal pauses for emphasis.

Trevon cannot imagine what the one condition could possibly be as he gives Jamaal his undivided attention.

Jamaal then goes on, "And that one condition is that you check in with me on a daily basis, as I said before; so that I *know* without a shadow of doubt that you and your family are okay. Trevon, man, we're going to get through this! We just have to remain strong and continue to be there for each other."

Trevon remains silent, thinking how much he secretly admires Jamaal's faith and confidence.

As they reach the school building, Jamaal turns to Trevon and tells him, "Man, believe me when I say that I know there is no easy solution to your family's dilemma. However, you best believe that we'll be working *very hard* on coming up with some answers." As Jamaal reflects on Trevon's life experience, he begins to recall sayings that have been instilled in him by his mother and grandmother. "I've always believed that 'if there's a will there's a way.' We have the *will* to make positive changes in our lives, and I know that we'll find the *way*," he confidently asserts.

Trevon is impressed by Jamaal's level of faith and maturity. He gazes at Jamaal while thinking about what life could be like for him and his siblings if he were able to pursue his passion for creating and producing music. As they approach the school building, Trevon begins to smile, as the thought of Jamaal graduating high school and going off to college crosses his mind. "Thanks, man! Your friendship and support means the world to me," he declares as he gives Jamaal a brotherly hug of love and support.

"Yeah, ditto; it's all good," replies Jamaal. He turns and leaps up the steps leading into the school building. "I'll see you tomorrow! You be safe, okay!" shouts Jamaal.

"Okay! Later, man—see you tomorrow!" Trevon shouts back. He thinks about his life experience and his conversation with Jamaal, as he walks away from the school building. He then jogs toward the park, where he spends the rest of the afternoon waiting for his brothers and sister to get out of school.

CHAPTER 5

COMMITTED TO CHANGE

It's Saturday morning. Jamaal and Trevon have planned to meet at the park next to Trevon's house at ten o'clock to discuss having their parents meet for the first time. Jamaal is very excited as he jumps out of bed and rushes to get dressed. He is especially excited about having his mother meet Trevon's mother.

Jamaal's mother is just as excited as he is about helping Trevon's family in any way possible. Jamaal has full confidence in his mother's ability to help Trevon's mother get her life back on track, and he is desperately hoping that Trevon will allow his mother to intervene as he races to the park where they are scheduled to meet.

Jamaal notices Trevon from a distance and calls out, "Hey, Trevon!"

Trevon yells back, "Hey, Jamaal! What's up?"

Jamaal jogs over to Trevon to greet him. He can tell that there is something troubling Trevon as he approaches him. "Hey, how's it going?"

"I don't know, man," states Trevon as he leans in to give Jamaal a handshake and a brotherly hug. Trevon is not in a very good mood, but he is excited to see Jamaal.

"Trevon, man, are you okay? Is everything all right?"

Trevon shakes his head from side to side as he angrily replies, "Jamaal, I really don't know. All I know is that *I'm tired*!"

"Tired?" questions Jamaal. "What's up, man? What happened?" He shakes his head from side to side while thinking that this is not like his friend. He declares, "You know that you can talk to me about anything, and I do mean anything."

Trevon wants to talk to Jamaal, but he does not know where to start. "Jamaal, you know the deal. Look at my life. All I know is that I'm sick and tired of living the way I've been living for the past fifteen years. I'm truly fed up!"

"Yeah, I know, but we agreed to have our parents meet so that my mother could help your mother. As I said before, I'm here for you, and I'm going to help you get through this. I don't care what it takes," Jamaal insists as he places his hand on Trevon's shoulder.

Trevon cautiously states, "Yeah, I know but—"

Jamaal is hoping that Trevon follows through with their plan to have their mothers meet, as he interrupts, "I know that it's tough on you, but we're going to get through this, and I mean it!"

"Yeah, I know." Trevon pauses and looks Jamaal in the eyes while firmly stating, "Jamaal, I know you mean well, but I can't go through with this. I can't have your mother meet my mother." Trevon begins to think about his mother's drug use, and he is unable to control his emotions as he lashes out. "It's just not worth it!"

Jamaal is taken aback by Trevon's angry tone and is afraid that Trevon is going to give up on their plan to get help for his mother. "Not worth it!" he cries out. "What do you mean, not worth it! Trevon, your mother needs help, and we're going to get her the help she needs, one way or another!"

Trevon tries to brush Jamaal off, glaring at him as he responds, "Jamaal, man, trust me when I say it's not worth it. It's not worth wasting your time—or your mother's time, for that matter. It's just not worth it! Mom will never change! She's not going to change." Trevon has witnessed his mother's altered state from using drugs almost every day over the past five years, and he seriously doubts that she will ever change. He looks at Jamaal, lets out an exasperated sigh, and firmly states, "Just trust me on this, okay? It's just not worth it. Can we just leave it at that?" he insists.

Jamaal has complete trust and confidence in his mother's ability to help Trevon and his family. He is determined to get them the support that they so desperately need. He will not let his friend back out. "No, Trevon," Jamaal tells him sternly. "We can't just leave it at that. I don't know what caused you to change your mind. However, I am *not* giving up on you *or* your mother. What is going on, man? What is with the attitude?" Jamaal huffs under his breath, shaking his head from side to side as he stares at the ground in frustration.

In realizing how determined and deeply involved Jamaal has become with his family's situation, Trevon cries out, "Okay! If you must know, I'm almost too embarrassed to have your mother meet my mother. All my mother cares about is getting high. And you know what? It's just not worth it! Can we just leave it at that?" he angrily insists.

Jamaal lets out a deep sigh of frustration. "Okay, I hear you, but that was the main reason for our parents meeting. The plan was to have my mom help your mother get help. Right?" Jamaal throws up his arms.

Trevon exasperatedly throws his hands up too in frustration, as he passionately shouts, "No, Jamaal! I know you care about me and my family, but you don't understand! *All*—and I do mean *all*—my mother cares about is getting high! It's almost as though she can't go a day without getting high. She doesn't even try to hide it anymore. Jamaal, I almost *lost it* when I saw her getting high last night!"

Jamaal's eyes widen, and he covers his mouth in shock, as he cries out, "Oh no! What happened?"

Trevon shakes his head from side to side. He regains his composure, looks Jamaal in the eyes, and calmly confides, "Man, I couldn't stand it when I looked in the kitchen and saw my mother getting high."

"Ah, man, I can't believe it," replies Jamaal in a faint whisper.

"Yeah, I know. It's hard for me to believe it myself." This was the first time Trevon had actually seen his mother in the act of preparing and using drugs. She had become a pro at hiding the drugs and the drug paraphernalia from Trevon and his siblings. The fact that she was oblivious to Trevon and his brother Matthew's presence in the living room was the proverbial final straw for Trevon. "You're not going to believe it, but Matthew and I were sitting in the living room watching TV when Mom came home last night. She dropped the keys on the floor and headed straight for the kitchen. I don't think she even noticed us sitting on the couch." Trevon's frustration begins to show as he cries out, "She went straight in the kitchen and started oiling up *right there* at the kitchen table! Man, she cares more about using drugs than she cares about her own kids. If she doesn't care about us, why should I care about her!"

Jamaal remains silent as he shakes his head from side to side in disbelief.

"My mother started using right there at the kitchen table," repeats Trevon as he drops his head in shame. "Never mind the fact that my brother and I were right there in the living room. I tried to distract Matthew so that he wouldn't see her." Trevon reflects on when he first learned that his mother was addicted to drugs. "Now that I think about it, I was around Matthew's age when I first heard members of my family call my mother a 'drug addict' and a 'crackhead.' It blew me away," he recalls with anger.

"Man, they would call my mother all kinds of names. But I never thought that she would start using right in front of us."

"Yeah, man, that's *deep*."

"I tell you, man, I almost lost it when I looked over and saw her getting high! It took everything within me to keep from going off on her. If Matthew wasn't sitting on the couch next to me, there's no telling what I would have done. I could feel the rage building up inside. You just don't know how *angry* I was starting to get."

"Yeah, man, *I feel you*! That's even more reason for us to make sure we get your mother the help she needs. I know you don't want anything bad to happen to her, and it's not too late. We can find her the help and support that she needs to get off drugs." Jamaal is convinced of his mother's ability to help Trevon and his family. He looks Trevon squarely in the eyes and adamantly states, "Trust me—I am convinced of that!"

Trevon begins to calm down as he comes to terms with the fact that Jamaal simply refuses to give up. "Yeah, I believe you." He shakes his head as he thinks about Jamaal's strong faith and determination. "Jamaal, man, I tell you what. I don't know how you've managed to stay so strong. I sure wish I had the confidence that you have when it comes to helping my mother get off drugs. I don't know, man; I'm at the point where I couldn't care less about what happens to her."

Jamaal remains silent while attempting to figure out how best to support Trevon through this tough time in his life.

Trevon looks him squarely in the eyes and firmly asserts, "Jamaal, you can't begin to imagine the pain and heartache that my mother has caused us." He then calmly states, "I often wonder if she even cares one bit."

Drawing on his spirituality, Jamaal hastily replies with deep conviction, "I hear you, man, but I'm holding on to my faith. I know that we can help your mother. All your mother has to do is give us a chance. My mother can still talk to her this afternoon."

Trevon is deeply moved by the fact that Jamaal refuses to give up on him and his family. He remains silent while reflecting on what a true friend Jamaal is proving to be. Trevon wants to believe that Jamaal's mother can help them. However, growing up in a household with a mother who has been addicted to drugs for as long as he can remember seems to be holding him back from accepting help. He turns to Jamaal, saying, "I'm telling you—all she cares about is getting high. How can we help her when that's *all* she knows how to do?"

"Trevon, man, there is hope," Jamaal confidently and emphatically replies. "And I know that we can help her. I don't care if that is *all* she knows how to do. You're her son, and we're going to help her get off drugs, so that she can be a mother to you and your brothers and sister. Man, I can truly say that there's *nothing like* a mother's love, and I'm not going to let you go through life without knowing that love. Trust me when I say this: we're going to get your mother help."

"Jamaal, I know you mean well. But I'm sick and tired of trying to take care of my mother," Trevon fumingly states as he brushes Jamaal off. "And the thanks I get is watching her do drugs right in front of my face!" Trevon throws his hands in the air while turning his back to Jamaal. "No thanks! I give up!" he cries out.

Jamaal positions himself in front of Trevon, attempting to get his attention. "Trevon, man, I know that you're upset, and I can't begin to imagine how you must feel," Jamaal states as he places his hand on Trevon's shoulder. "But I know that you don't want to see your mom continue to waste her life away. She's your mother."

Trevon angrily yells out, "What mother! She has never been a mother to me nor any of us! The only mother I have ever known was my grandmother. And she died five years ago. As far as I'm concerned, I don't have a mother!"

Jamaal is speechless. Silence fills the air.

Trevon begins to calm down as he realizes that he is unfairly taking his anger out on Jamaal. As he fights back the tears, he expresses, "Jamaal, man, you just don't know how much pain my mother has caused us." Trevon buries his face in his hands as he begins to weep. He reflects on Jamaal's comments as he regains his composure. "Maybe you're right." he admits as he wipes the tears from his eyes. "Maybe I do love my mother. But to be honest with you, I don't even know what it means to love truly my mother, or anybody else for that matter. What I do know is that deep down in my heart I'm so afraid that drugs are going to get the best of her, and my worst nightmare will come true."

Jamaal remains silent as he listens intently to Trevon talking about his experience in growing up with a mother who has become addicted to drugs.

Trevon's voice begins to crack as he looks up and states, "Jamaal, man, you cannot begin to imagine the pain that I've had to go through. All in the name of having a *poor excuse* for a mother!" Trevon thinks about how he used to have nightmares about his mother and her drug use, to the point where he would wake up in the middle of the night, frightened to death that she had overdosed. He would leap out of his bed and race through the house, searching for his mother, and she would be nowhere to be found. He had often stayed up throughout the night, staring out the window while waiting for her to come home, fearing that the worst had happened. Trevon is no longer able to hold back his resentment toward his mother as he cries out, "I've had it with my mother's drug abuse. I'm out!"

Jamaal remains silent as he begins to silently pray to God for answers on how to help his best friend through this challenging time in his life.

Trevon shakes his head as he begins to think about how much he misses his grandmother. He looks Jamaal squarely in the eyes and solemnly states, "Jamaal, you can't begin to imagine what it's been like trying to make it in this life without having a family to turn to for support."

Jamaal is on the verge of tears as he listens to his best friend pour his heart out. He places his hand on Trevon's shoulder while trying hard to fight back the tears as he attempts to console him. "It's going to be okay. Man, I had no idea. Maybe now is not a good time to have our parents meet."

Trevon slowly shakes his head from side to side. "I know that it would be a good idea, but maybe I'm the one who's not ready."

"Yeah, I understand. It's okay," Jamaal compassionately states as he gives Trevon a brotherly hug. Jamaal is searching for a way to cheer Trevon up. He has an idea. Trevon could spend the day at his house with him and his mom! The smile on Jamaal's face broadens as he looks at Trevon and enthusiastically shares his idea, "Hey Trevon, how would you like to spend the day at my house with me and Mom?" His excitement heightens as he thinks about Trevon spending the day with him and his mother. "I'm sure Mom would love to have you over," he confidently declares.

Trevon is both excited and relieved by Jamaal's proposal. "Yeah, I think that would be a better idea," he calmly states. "I don't think I could stand being at home right now. I can definitely use the time to clear my head. I can't even look at my mother without getting upset about what happened last night." Trevon wants to accept Jamaal's invitation, but then he realizes that he can't when he thinks about his siblings. "I would love to spend the day with you and your mother, but I can't leave my brothers and our baby sister home alone with my mother."

"Hey, bring them over as well," Jamaal exuberantly replies. "We can all go out and have fun."

Trevon is relieved and excitedly replies, "Thanks, Jamaal. That sounds great! I'll go and get them and meet you at your house around noon."

Jamaal and Trevon exchange handshakes as they prepare to head home in opposite directions.

Trevon begins to fantasize about what it would be like to trade places with Jamaal for a day. As he starts to head home to get his siblings dressed to spend the day with Jamaal and his mother, he shouts, "I'll see you in a few!"

"You bet!" yells Jamaal as he jogs off in the opposite direction.

CHAPTER 6

IN THE VILLAGE

Jamaal enjoys the gentle breeze of the wind as he jogs toward his house. He is shocked to learn of all that Trevon is going through, and he is so pleased that he is able to openly talk with his mother about his friendship with Trevon. He begins to think about how blessed he is to have a mother and grandmother who genuinely care about him, in spite of his shortcomings. He then begins to think about all the times that he has taken his mother's love for granted. Jamaal realizes that at times he has been mean, angry, and disrespectful toward his mother—after all that she has done for him. He is so glad that she hasn't given up on him and that they have such a great relationship. Jamaal decides that he is going to give his mother a great big hug for all that she has done for him and for not giving up on him when he needed her the most.

I'd better hurry home to make sure that it's okay for Trevon and his brothers and sister to spend the day with me and Mom, he thinks to himself as he looks down at his watch. Jamaal is excited about talking with his mother about his meeting with Trevon, and he begins to sprint down the street to his house. He is convinced that his mother will be excited to have Trevon and his siblings spending the day with them. He races through the front door in search of his mother. "Mom, I'm home! Mom, where are you?" he calls out.

Marlene steps into the hall, leans over the balcony, and loudly replies, "I'm upstairs." She then slowly walks back to her room.

The smile on Jamaal's face broadens as he races upstairs and runs into his mother's room. He gives her a great big hug and a kiss on the cheek. He immediately begins to share his experience in meeting with Trevon. "Mom, you know how I've been telling you about my friend Trevon? I just got back from meeting with him, and we had a long talk about him and his mother."

Marlene's eyes widen as she responds. "Oh my, is his mother okay?" she asks, with her eyes remaining fixed on Jamaal.

"Well, kind of, sort of," Jamaal hesitantly says as he thinks about Trevon's mother.

"Jamaal, sweetheart, what do you mean?"

Jamaal is unable to contain his emotions as he anxiously cries out, "Mom, you're not going to believe it, but Trevon saw his mother getting high last night!"

Marlene shakes her head from side to side in disbelief. She can't understand how parents could have such a drug habit, to the point where they are oblivious to the needs of their children. Marlene notices the look of concern on Jamaal's face as she lets out an exasperated sigh. "I know that that must have been tough on Trevon. How is he?"

"He's much better now, but it really upset him," Jamaal tells her.

Marlene is relieved to know that Trevon is doing okay in light of his experience, and she replies, "Yes, I'm sure it did."

"Momma, Trevon and I talked at length about his mother, and he decided that he was not ready for his mother to meet with you."

Jamaal's mother is a practicing attorney who worked as a substance abuse counselor prior to obtaining her law degree. She had been looking forward to meeting with Trevon's mother, in hopes of getting her to commit to entering a residential substance abuse treatment program. She is disappointed but does not let it show.

"Yes, I was looking forward to meeting with Trevon's mother, but I do understand. You know that I would do anything within my power to help Trevon and his family."

"Yes, Mom, I know. That's what I told Trevon, but seeing his mother getting high really upset him."

"Did he say anything to her?" Marlene inquires. She is deeply committed to helping Trevon and his family, and she is quite pleased that Jamaal is comfortable talking with her about all that Trevon and his family are going through.

"No, Trevon said that she didn't even notice him and his younger brother sitting in the living room watching TV. She just rushed into the house and headed straight for the kitchen. Momma, Trevon was *so* upset! I could tell that it was still bothering him, so I suggested that he and his brothers and baby sister come over and spend the day with us."

"Oh, sweetheart, that would be great!"

Jamaal smiles as he asserts, "Yeah. I was hoping you wouldn't mind."

"No, not at all!"

The doorbell rings before Jamaal can respond. He suspects that it might be Trevon already. "I'll get it!" he calls out as he leaps to his feet.

"Okay," states Marlene.

Jamaal rushes downstairs to answer the door. He swings the door open and cries out, "Hey, Trevon, that was fast!"

"Yeah, I figured I would get my brothers and sister ready and leave right away," Trevon replies. His baby sister is joyfully tugging at his arm.

"Great! Now we can have the whole day to hang out. I'll let Mom know that you're here."

Trevon playfully pushes his little sister's hand from his forearm as he replies, "Okay."

Jamaal runs upstairs to let his mother know that Trevon and his siblings have arrived.

"Okay, tell them I'll be right down," Marlene excitedly states.

Jamaal rushes back downstairs and does just that.

"Thanks, man." Trevon's love for his siblings begins to show as he announces, "Oh, let me introduce you to my younger brothers and our little sister." He turns to his siblings and points them out one by one: "This is Matthew. He's ten, and this is Jalen. He just turned eight last week."

"Hey, Matthew, and happy belated birthday, Jalen," Jamaal says with a smile.

Jalen says, "Thank you," with a beaming smile.

"And this is Tyrell. He's six and a half, and this is our baby sister, Marla. She just turned five," states Trevon as he playfully pulls Marla to his side.

Jamaal leans down to greet Marla. "Hey, Marla, my name is Jamaal. Can I have a high five?"

Marla smiles as she gives Jamaal a high five.

"Hey, let's go downstairs in the basement and hang out until Mom gets ready," suggests Jamaal, turning to Trevon and his siblings. He beckons for them to follow him. With Jamaal leading the way, Trevon and his siblings head downstairs. Jamaal gives Marla crayons and a piece of paper to draw on while Matthew, Jalen, and Tyrell watch as he and Trevon play video games on the big screen TV.

An hour has passed and Jamaal's mother is ready to take everyone out for the afternoon. She opens the basement door and calls out to Jamaal. "Jamaal, are you guys ready to head out?"

Jamaal turns to Trevon and his siblings and exuberantly informs them, "Hey, you guys. Mom's ready." He walks over to the bottom of the stairs and respectfully yells out, "Yes, ma'am—we're coming!"

Marla and Tyrell lead the way as they scurry up the stairs.

Marlene greets them as they reach the top of the stairs. She loves children, and she is excited about taking the little ones to Chuck E. Cheese; she shares her plans to drop Trevon and Jamaal off at the movies. They leap with joy as she informs them of how the day will be spent.

As they are walking out the door, the phone rings. "I'll get that," Marlene says. She turns to Jamaal. "Here, Jamaal, take the keys. You guys can wait in the car. I'll be right out."

"Come on, guys. Let's go." Jamaal beckons to Trevon and his siblings. As they head to the car, the thought of having Trevon and his siblings spend the night and attend church with him and his mother crosses Jamaal's mind. "Hey, Trevon, how would you guys like to spend the night?" he excitedly asks. "You can stay over and go to church with us in the morning."

Trevon has not seen the inside of a church since his grandmother passed away. "Wow, that would be great," he enthusiastically replies. Trevon smiles as he reflects on his love for his grandmother. He then begins to wonder whether it will be okay with Jamaal's mother. "Are you sure your mom won't mind?" he cautiously asks.

"Of course not," Jamaal confidently asserts. "I'm sure she wouldn't mind. If anything, she'll be excited. After the movies and Chuck E. Cheese, we can stop by your house and make sure that it's okay with your mother."

Trevon chuckles in disbelief. "Jamaal, man, are you serious?" he sarcastically exclaims. "Nobody has ever mentioned checking anything out with my mom. We're on our own. We take care of ourselves." In thinking about how he has raised himself and is now raising his younger siblings, Trevon boldly states, "If anything, I look out for my younger brothers and our baby sister." He chuckles as he thinks about how oblivious his mother seems to be to the world around her. He humorously comments, "We could stay out for a week, and my mother wouldn't even know that we were missing."

Jamaal compassionately replies, "Yeah, but you never know. If your mom's home when we get there, we can let her know that you guys will be spending the night. I'll ask my mom about it when she gets in the car, but I'm positive that she's going to say yes." Jamaal smiles as he lightheartedly states, "Mom *loves* taking people to church. I don't think there's anything Mom loves more than going to church." Jamaal then begins to think about his grandmother as he looks Trevon in the eyes. "Hey, you may even get to meet my grandmother. We all go to the same church."

Marlene comes out to the car, gets into the driver's seat, and buckles her seat belt. She turns to Jamaal and smiles. "I needed to take that call," she says. She then turns to Trevon and his siblings and smiles at them in turn. "Are you guys ready for a fun-filled afternoon?" she asks.

"Yes, ma'am! We're ready," Jamaal excitedly proclaims, with a glowing smile on his face. "But Mom," he coyly states, "there's something we need to ask you on the way to the movies." Jamaal's grin widens as he glances at Trevon in the back seat.

"Okay," replies Marlene as she instructs everyone to buckle up. She is excited about Jamaal having a friend that he genuinely cares for. She glances in the back seat at Trevon and his siblings and gives them a big, warm, welcoming smile. "We're ready to go," she warmly announces as she puts the car in reverse and starts to back out of the garage.

Chapter 7

UNDYING LOVE

Jamaal's excitement in having Trevon and his siblings spend the night has prevented him from sleeping in. It's just six thirty, and he's already awake. Jamaal has been thinking more and more about his father, and he wonders whether today would be a good day to talk with his mother about his feelings toward him. He jumps out of bed and checks around to see if anyone else is awake. He looks down the hall and notices that his mother's bedroom door is partially open. Knowing that his mom sleeps with her door closed, he decides that she must be up. He peeks inside—and sees Marla at the head of the bed, sound asleep. He smiles. He is thinking to himself that his mom is probably in the kitchen, cooking breakfast.

Jamaal dashes downstairs, nearly tripping over his own feet. He races into the kitchen to greet his mother. "Good morning, Mom." He is breathing heavily as he attempts to catch his breath.

"Good morning, sweetheart. You're up bright and early," Marlene replies with a smile.

"Yes, I'm very excited about Trevon and his brothers and sister coming to church with us today." These thoughts cause Jamaal to think about how things used to be when his dad was around and the times that they had attended church together as a family.

"So am I."

Jamaal looks up at his mother and asks, "Do you need any help?"

"That's very nice of you to ask. But I think I'm good. Are you the only one up?" she asks, with a loving smile on her face.

"Yes, I believe so. I looked in and saw that Marla was still asleep. I know Tyrell was still sleeping in the bed next to me when I got up."

Marlene gives Jamaal an affectionate look and asks, "How would you like to be in charge of making sure everyone is up and ready by eight thirty? As they wake up, you can show them around and make sure they're all able to find what they need."

"Okay. That's easy," Jamaal enthusiastically replies. "I can do that. When should I start waking them up?" he asks as he looks up at the clock.

"Hmm, let's see." Marlene is pensive, hand on chin. "Around seven-thirty should be good. You can wake the oldest two up first, giving them enough time to get dressed before waking up the little ones. That way everyone should be dressed and ready to eat breakfast by eight-thirty."

"Okay, I'll go ahead and get dressed, since I'm already up." Jamaal hesitates—. He is preoccupied with thoughts about his dad, and he desperately wants to talk with his mother about his feelings toward his father. However, he is not sure how his mother feels about his dad, and he doesn't want to ruin the day by bringing up the topic.

"Yes, sweetheart, that sounds like a great idea," Marlene concludes.

As Jamaal prepares to head upstairs to get dressed, he continues to think about his dad and wonder about discussing him with his mother. He is unable to make up his mind. He turns around and calls out to his mom. "Oh, Mom, I forgot to tell you something."

Marlene turns to look in his direction. "Yes, dear? What is it?"

With a tender smile, Jamaal tells her, "I love you."

Marlene blushes as she warmly replies, "I love you too dear."

As Jamaal turns to head upstairs, he is still thinking about his father, and so he decides to go back into the kitchen to talk with his mother. He does not know where to begin as he seeks to get her attention. "Mom, you know what?"

"No, what is it, dear?"

Jamaal opens the conversation by talking about his relation-ship with Trevon while deep down inside he is thinking about how much he misses his dad. "I can't help thinking about Trevon. I think about him all the time. I think about him at night before going to bed and then again when I wake up in the morning."

Marlene takes his comments at face value. "Yes, dear, the two of you are pretty close, and with all that Trevon is going through, it is only natural that you're going to think about him."

"Yeah, but knowing Trevon has really helped me grow to love and appreciate you and Grandma. I know that we've had our ups and downs over the past year, but I never knew how good I had it until meeting Trevon and coming to realize all that he has had to go through."

"Yes, sweetheart, we all go through our struggles in life. Believe me, life can be full of ups and downs."

Feeling reassured of his mother's love for him, Jamaal musters up the strength to share his true feelings regarding his father's absence, as he fixes his eyes on his mother. "Yeah, I know, and I don't know what I would do without you and Grandma. But Mom, I often wish that Dad were around. In looking at Trevon's situation, I realize I've got it good, and I know I shouldn't be complaining, but I miss Dad a lot. I'm not as upset with him as I used to be, but I sure wish he would call."

Marlene empathizes with Jamaal while silently wishing once more that his father would show some interest in him by at least picking up the phone to call. She lets out a long sigh, gazes at her son, and says, "Yes, dear, I know. Believe me, I have not stopped praying that your dad will one day call and make the commitment to be actively involved in your life." Marlene is just as puzzled as Jamaal by his father's absence. She wonders what could possibly be preventing him from making contact with Jamaal. "Yes, we have managed without him, but you deserve to have him play an active role in your life. But trust me when I say that he's the one who is missing out on the blessing of knowing you as his son. Your father can't begin to imagine how great the loss has been for the *both* of you. I just regret that he has not come to realize how much he has missed out on over the past four years."

"Momma, do you think I'll ever get to see my father again?" Jamaal inquires. "I miss him *so much*! I wish that he were a part of my life."

"Baby, I know." Marlene pauses as she reflects on her son's comment. "Sweetheart, I honestly don't have the answer, but I certainly hope so. I wish I could tell you that your father *definitely* will be a part of your life at some point in the future and be right." Because she lost her father when she was five years of age, Marlene understands Jamaal's desire to have his father in his life. She spontaneously offers, "If you are interested, we can begin a search for your father and try to find him. However, I would not want you to get your hopes up and be disappointed."

Jamaal feels reassured by his mother's love and understanding of his desire to reconnect with his father. "Yes, ma'am; I understand," he warmly replies. "But I do think about him a lot," he confides.

"Yes, I'm sure you do," Marlene lovingly affirms. "I think about him a lot myself. I hope he's okay. I often wish that he would call, if for no other reason but to let us know that he's okay. Believe me, I would love for you to have a relationship with your father, and that's the honest-to-God truth. He's your father and will always be." Marlene seeks acknowledgment as she looks Jamaal in the eyes. "Okay?" she asks.

Jamaal nods as he solemnly replies, "Yes, I know."

Sensing Jamaal's sadness, Marlene attempts to reassure him that she has not, to her knowledge, done anything to prevent his father from contacting the family. "Sweetheart, our number has not changed, and it's up to your father to make the call. Should he call, I would gladly welcome him into our lives to be as involved with you as he would like to be. I know that we're divorced, but there are no hard feelings."

"Thanks, Mom. That means a lot to me." Jamaal is encouraged by his mother's positive comments.

"You're welcome, sweetheart." Marlene reaches over to give him a warm hug. Several thoughts go through her mind concerning her ex-husband not making contact with her or Jamaal. She begins to ask herself, *Could he possibly be remarried? Could that be why he has not made contact with me or Jamaal? Is he in a new long-term relationship? Does he have other children that he is taking care of while completely ignoring his responsibilities in taking care of Jamaal?*

Jamaal warmly embraces his mother and breathes a sigh of relief at knowing that she still cares for his father. He slowly releases his embrace. He looks up at the clock and loudly exclaims, "I had better go get dressed! It's getting late."

Marlene smiles as she replies, "Okay, dear." Her smile broadens as she watches Jamaal bounce up the stairs. She continues to think about Jamaal's father and concludes that they will never know what is keeping him from contacting the family, unless he just happens to call them out of the blue.

At the top of the stairs, Jamaal peeks his head inside the guest bedroom. He notices that Trevon is up and exuberantly states, "Hey, you're up!"

"Yeah. Good morning."

"Good morning, Tre. How'd you sleep?"

"Man, I tell you what, I slept like a rock." Trevon cannot recall the last time he has gotten a good night's rest without worrying about his mother, brothers, baby sister, or members of his crew.

"That's good. I didn't think that anyone else was awake," Jamaal states as they spontaneously head to Jamaal's room.

"Yeah, I just got up about five minutes ago. Truth be told, I rarely ever sleep more than three to four hours a night. But it sure was good to sleep for almost seven and a half hours straight."

"That's good to hear. You, me, and Mom, we're the only ones up so far. Mom is downstairs fixing breakfast. You're not going to believe it, but we were just downstairs talking about *my dad*," states Jamaal as he chuckles under his breath.

"Really?" asks Trevon in disbelief.

"Yes, for real! Hard to believe, huh? I was just telling Mom about how much I miss my dad and how I wish that he was a part of my life. You know, I often wonder if I will ever get to see my dad again."

"Yeah, I know what you mean. I can definitely relate."

"Speaking of which, you are going to follow up in talking with your mother about our plans to have her meet with my mom, *right*?" Jamaal is hoping to get an affirmative response from Trevon, as he silently awaits his reply.

"Jamaal, you know I do love my mother, and I want to see her get better. But she's been using drugs for *too many* years," argues Trevon as he tries to dodge the question. "She'll *never* change. As you know, my grandmother was the only real mother that I've ever known. And since my grandmother's death, man, I've been trying *so hard* to save my mother, but I must admit things have not gotten any better."

"Yeah, I know. But I'm glad that you didn't give up on yourself *or* your mother way back when. And you know what? I'm not going to let you give up *now*. There is hope for your mother, and we're going to help her find that hope one way or another. I mean that!"

Trevon reluctantly gives in to Jamaal's persistence. "You know what, Jamaal? I truly do hope that we can help her find that help real soon, because life is too short." Trevon shakes his head from side to side while reflecting on his mother's longstanding drug use. "I can't continue to live my life worrying about my mother day in and day out. I have my own hopes and dreams that I need to pursue—with or without her."

Jamaal is excited to hear Trevon refer to his hopes and dreams. He enthusiastically replies, "Yeah, I hear you! Man, Trevon, you have *big* hopes and dreams that I *know* will come true." Jamaal playfully pokes Trevon on the shoulder while jokingly adding, "And look here, when you blow up, don't you forget about me!" Jamaal pats his chest while commenting, "I'm your boy, and I'm going to be riding your coattail all the way to the top. It's going to be you and me, ride or die, the legit way."

Trevon smiles as he playfully grabs Jamaal around the neck and puts him in a loose headlock. "Not a chance! You know that you're my boy and always will be. We're blood brothers for life," he declares.

"Trevon, man, it's so good to see you smile," expresses Jamaal. He then slyly shifts the conversation back to Trevon's mother. "Now, when would be a good time for my mother to meet with you and your mom?"

Trevon was hoping that Jamaal would change the topic completely; he is trying to avoid thinking about his mother. However, realizing that Jamaal is not going to give up on the idea, he concedes. "You're going to be there too, right?" he asks.

"Sure, of course! If you would like for me to be, then I'm there, without a doubt!"

"Yes, most definitely, I am *not* planning to be there unless you're there. Sad to say, but I can't stand to be around my mother right now."

"Yeah, man, I totally understand. I felt the same way about my mother when she was riding my back like crazy, and we were constantly getting into heated arguments and fights. Man, I thank God we made it through that madness."

Trevon has a sad smile on his face as he thinks about how Jamaal has been sheltered and protected from the streets. He realizes that Jamaal cannot begin to imagine what it's like to have a parent addicted to drugs. He has no idea what it's like to live so close to the destructive world of drugs, a world where one cares more about feeding one's need than about feeding the children. Trevon realizes that Jamaal has not had to witness his mother's struggle to pay rent or buy the basic necessities like food and clothing. He also knows that Jamaal has no idea what it is like to go without eating for days at a time, to miss a meal out of necessity. Trevon shakes his head from side to side while secretly admiring the comfortable lifestyle that Jamaal seems to have, a lifestyle he wishes he could experience, if only for a day.

Jamaal remains focused on his desire to get help for Trevon and his family as he passionately states, "Man, we don't have much time to waste in getting your mom the help she needs. You think she will meet with us this coming weekend?" he asks Trevon.

Trevon thinks about his mother's unpredictable behavior and

then scornfully replies, "Huh, it's hard to tell. I don't know what goes on inside my mother's head. She could agree to meet and then, when the time comes, she can end up being nowhere to be found."

Jamaal remains confident in his mother's ability to help. "Okay, I tell you what," he proposes. "Maybe my mom and I can come over first thing Saturday morning." Jamaal pauses as he turns to Trevon and asks, "What time does your mother get up?"

Trevon pauses while trying to figure out when that would be. "Hmm, I would say she gets up on average around one or two o'clock in the afternoon." He thinks about her pattern while commenting, "Truth be told, she doesn't get in some mornings until two or three o'clock."

"Okay," Jamaal insists. "Here's the plan. My mom and I will meet you at your house around eleven-thirty Saturday morning. You can plan to have your brothers and sister up and dressed by then. We can start the family meeting around twelve noon." The thought of inviting other family members crosses Jamaal's mind, so he excitedly asks, "Are there any other relatives, or friends, that we can invite to be a part of the family meeting?"

"Let me see. I'm not sure," replies Trevon. He ponders who his mother knows. He then thinks about one of his mother's closest friends. "Oh, my mother does have a good friend named Lauren, who she has known since high school. Lauren used to call and come by the house all the time." Trevon pauses as he reflects on the fact that he has not seen Lauren in quite some time. "Now that I think about it, Lauren has not called or visited with my mother in over a year. But I know where she lives. I can stop by her house tomorrow and see if she'll be able to meet with us on Saturday."

"Okay, that would be great! Oh, I almost forgot that I told my grandmother I would spend time with her this coming weekend. Maybe she can join us. I'm sure she would love to help." Jamaal smiles as he passionately states, "My mother and grandmother are *so much* alike."

Trevon is amazed by Jamaal's family. He chuckles as he enviously remarks, "Man, you've got it made."

"Yeah, Trevon, you're right—and I'm beginning to realize just how much!"

Trevon looks Jamaal in the eyes while shaking his head from side to side. "Man, I would love to trade places with you." Trevon begins to tease Jamaal as he raises his head to look up at the ceiling. He then mimics a snobbish British accent: "If I had *your* life, I would be excelling in school, a *top* athlete nonetheless, and on my way to receiving a *full* scholarship to the Juilliard School, with a special interest in their Center for Innovation in the *Arts*, nonetheless." Trevon pauses as he sternly looks Jamaal in the eyes. There is a slight hint of envy as he flippantly continues, "Oh my, what a life I would be living …"

Jamaal chuckles inwardly as Trevon makes light of his upper middle class lifestyle. He finds Trevon's dramatic parody to be quite humorous as he interrupts. "Hold up," he snappily retorts. "As you know, 'Life for me ain't been no crystal stair.' Things have not necessarily been easy for me. And need I remind you that my mom and I have had our fair share of ups and downs?"

Trevon smiles while admiring Jamaal's tenacity. "Yeah, I know," he admits. "But still, it is ten thousand times better than my life. Jamaal, man, you and your mother have a *good* relationship—you can sit down and actually *talk* with each other. And you know what? I can't remember the last time my mother and I sat down to talk about anything." Trevon becomes animated as he begins to mock his relationship with his mother. "I can see myself walking up to my mother trying to talk to her and have her look me *dead* in the face and say, 'Excuse me, but do I know you?' 'Who *are* you?'" Trevon uses humor to make light of his fractured relationship with his mother. "She'll be like, 'Excuse me, but whose child *are* you?' 'Where did you come from?'"

Jamaal chuckles under his breath. "Man, you have a mad sense of humor. Trevon, man, you keep me smiling. That's what I like most about you. You don't let life get you down, no matter how difficult things may get. You tend to keep your head up, and that's a good thing."

Trevon becomes more serious as he states, "Jamaal, to be honest with you, I don't even know *how* to go about letting my mother know that you and your family will be coming over on Saturday. I can't remember the last time my mother and I have looked each other in the face. And I don't think that we have ever sat down to actually have a real conversation about anything, ever."

"Okay, okay. I get it. But look here. You can tell her that special company will be coming over on Saturday to meet with her. If she asks who the company is, tell her that it's a surprise. My mother can take it from there."

Trevon smirks as he sarcastically comments, "Yeah, I'm *sure* she'll go for that. She loves it when she's the center of attention. But Jamaal, man, I just hope my mother follows through. I would hate to have you and your mother go through the trouble of setting up a family meeting and my mother's a no-show."

Jamaal understands Trevon's concerns, and he replies, "No worries. We've got this." Jamaal looks at the clock. Realizing how much time has passed, he turns to Trevon and exclaims, "Oh my! We've got to get ready for church."

"Looks like Matthew and Jalen are up. I hear them laughing and playing in the room next door," says Trevon.

After taking their showers and getting dressed, Jamaal, Trevon, and his siblings head downstairs for breakfast. They eat together, like a family, and head to church.

The church service is very moving and quite emotional for

Trevon, given the fact that the message touches on issues related to loss and abandonment. Jamaal, also, becomes teary eyed during the sermon.

As the service comes to an end and the offer is extended for persons to accept Christ into their lives, Trevon seriously thinks about receiving Christ as Lord and Savior of his life, but he decides to remain in his seat because he does not want his brothers and sister to be left behind. He is not sure what it would mean for him to become a member of Jamaal's church without his brothers and baby sister joining as well. He also begins to wonder whether he would be able to make it to church on a regular basis, given the fact that the church is in the suburbs and is a good distance from his home.

Afterward, Jamaal and his mother turn to greet and shake hands with fellow church members. While doing so, Jamaal's mother makes it a point to introduce Trevon, Matthew, Tyrell, Jalen, and Marla to various members of the church, including Pastor Lynell and First Lady Isabelle.

Trevon feels good about the day. He especially enjoyed the youth choir, as they melodically sang contemporary gospel songs that he is familiar with.

As they prepare to head to the car, Marlene turns to Jamaal, Trevon, and his siblings and asks, "Are you guys about ready to go?"

"Yes, ma'am. We're all here," replies Jamaal.

"Okay, I figured we'd go out for dinner. I'm sure you are all pretty hungry by now," states Marlene with a smile.

"Yes, we sure are!" shouts Jamaal as his stomach begins to growl.

Trevon warmly states, "Yes, ma'am."

Matthew is excited about going out to dinner, and he enthusiastically exclaims, "Ms. Marlene, you're the greatest!"

Jalen and Tyrell respond in like manner. "Yes, Ms. Marlene, you sure are!"

"I wish our mother was like you," Marla innocently states as she looks up at Jamaal's mother.

Marlene leans over and whispers in Marla's ear. "Oh, that is *so sweet*. But I know that you have a *wonderful* mother, and I can't *wait* to meet her." Marlene kisses Marla on the forehead and lovingly comments, "And, Marla sweetheart, always know that you and your brothers are sweet and precious children of a very loving and faithful God, who I know will continue to take good care of you and your family."

Marla smiles as she gazes into Marlene's eyes with a sense of pride and confidence while nodding her head in agreement.

Marlene turns to Trevon and his siblings and tells them, "I will drop you guys off at home after dinner, so you can get ready for school tomorrow." In realizing that she forgot to inquire about homework, she turns to Jamaal and Trevon, covers her mouth, and cries out, "Oh my! I failed to ask if you guys had any homework."

Matthew enthusiastically states, "Not me."

"Not me," says Jalen.

Tyrell chimes in, "Me neither."

Marla coyly states, "I don't have any homework either."

"Doesn't seem like any one of the little ones had homework. Marlene turns to Jamaal and inquisitively asks, "And what about you and Trevon?"

"No, ma'am. I don't have any homework," Trevon immediately replies.

"And what about you Jamaal?" Marlene asks as she awaits his reply.

"I finished all of my homework on Friday," Jamaal confidently states with a smile.

"Okay, that's good," declares Marlene. "So I don't feel bad

Muriel Kennedy, PhD

about keeping you out all weekend." Marlene decides to take everybody to the new upscale restaurant that has opened up around the corner from the university where she and Jamaal's father attended undergraduate school. Following dinner, she gives the kids a tour of her alma mater before dropping Trevon and his siblings off at their house.

"Okay, we're here," Marlene states as she pulls into Trevon's driveway and puts the car in park. "You guys have a wonderful evening, and I will see you soon."

Trevon gets out and stands next to the car, watching his siblings as they shuffle across the back seat to get out.

Marlene turns to Trevon and warmly states, "It was great having you and your siblings spend the day with us. And I want you to feel free to call or come by the house any time you like. Okay?"

"Yes, ma'am," he slowly replies. "And thank you once again for everything." Trevon is humbled by Marlene's love and support.

"You are *quite* welcome," insists Marlene. She looks on as Trevon's siblings exit the car one by one and admires how attentive Trevon is to the needs of the younger ones. Jalen, Tyrell and Marla rush over to give Marlene a hug while thanking her for allowing them to spend the night.

In experiencing the warmth of Marlene's love toward him and his siblings, Trevon turns to her and states, "Oh, Ms. Marlene, Jamaal and I talked this morning. And we decided to have you meet with my mother this coming Saturday, if that's okay with you."

"Oh, that would be *great!*" Marlene enthusiastically proclaims with a broad smile. "Meeting this coming Saturday sounds like a great idea. I'm looking forward to meeting your mother."

Trevon humbly confides, "Yes, ma'am. I'm looking forward to you and my mother meeting as well." With his siblings gathered at his side, Trevon continues, "Ms. Marlene, we appreciate your allowing us to spend the night and taking us to church and out to dinner. You don't know how much that meant to us. We have not had this much fun in our entire life. Jamaal is blessed to have you as a mother."

Matthew chimes in with great excitement, "Yeah, thank you, Ms. Marlene. We had so much fun."

Jalen, Tyrell, and Marla melodiously respond all at once, "Thanks, Ms. Marlene."

Marlene is deeply moved by all the children's expressions of appreciation as she lovingly replies, "You are so very welcome, and I do look forward to us hanging out again soon." Marlene smiles as she bids Trevon and his siblings a good night.

"Good night, Ms. Marlene," Trevon warmly states. He turns to Jamaal next. "Good night, Jamaal."

"Good night, Tre."

Marlene is smiling with joy as she watches Trevon and his siblings walk toward the front of the house.

As Trevon reaches the front door, Jamaal yells out, "Hey, Trevon! I'll give you a call tomorrow night. Okay?"

"Okay, sounds good. Good night. We really had a great time!" Trevon shouts back.

"We'll see you on Saturday," Marlene confidently calls out, as she waves to Trevon and his siblings. She watches them enter the house. As she prepares to back out of the driveway, she turns to Jamaal and warmly states, "Those are some fine young fellows and the most adorable little girl." She thinks to herself, *I know their mother loves them dearly.* She then wonders aloud, "How could she not?"

Jamaal remains silent as he thinks about what it would be like if Trevon's mother was actively involved in her children's lives.

Marlene notices that Jamaal is deep in thought. She glances over at him with great love and admiration as he continues to stare out the window. Marlene gently pats him on the shoulder while commenting, "Your friend Trevon is truly amazing."

"Yes, Mom. He sure is," agrees Jamaal as he looks in his mother's direction. "I told Grandma all about how Trevon and I first met. I have not told you yet, but I'm looking forward to telling you, now that we are able to talk again. I've really missed talking with you, Mom," Jamaal lovingly states.

"Yes, son, and I have missed our talks as well," Marlene says with affection. She is touched by Jamaal's compassionate heart and looks forward to spending time with him now that she has cut back on her hours at work. She smiles as she tells him, "We're going to have lots of time to talk. And I'm looking forward to spending quality time with the *most important* person in my life."

Jamaal smiles as he rests his head on his mother's shoulder.

Marlene gently pats Jamaal on the top of his head while keeping her eyes on the road. "Yes, it will be you and me, son; just you and me. We will be able to spend as much time as you like talking about all the things that you would like to talk about—with no interruptions."

Jamaal's smile broadens as he takes a deep breath. He closes his eyes and begins to think about how much he loves his mother and grandmother.

CHAPTER 8

SAVING GRACE

Jamaal and Trevon have been in touch throughout the week. Jamaal, his mother, and his grandmother are scheduled to meet at Trevon's house on Saturday. Jamaal is anxious to find out how Trevon's conversation went with his mother. He is hoping and praying that nothing interferes with their plan to have their mothers meet. Jamaal invites Trevon to stop by his house on Friday after school so that they can go over their plan for the next day. Trevon willingly agrees.

Friday afternoon, Trevon is in a very good mood as he heads over to Jamaal's house. He arrives around four-thirty and rings the doorbell.

Jamaal is anxiously awaiting his arrival. His excitement heightens as he hears the doorbell and rushes to answer. He swings the door open and loudly exclaims, "Hey, Trevon, come on in! We can go up to my room."

"Sure, man."

As they head upstairs, Jamaal is unable to contain his excitement. "So, how did it go?" he enthusiastically asks.

"So far so good," Trevon states, crossing his fingers. He then begins to relate the unusual experience that he had with his mother. "You're not going to believe it, but Mom made it home around eleven-thirty last night. And I actually talked with her about you and your mother and a couple other people coming over tomorrow." Trevon's eyes widen as he asks incredulously, "Can you believe that?"

Jamaal remains silent while giving Trevon his undivided attention.

"Mom actually said that it would be *fine* to have your mother and a couple other people come over tomorrow. She seemed to be looking forward to meeting with your mother. I could not believe it!" Trevon exclaims. "I just hope she follows through and does not do anything embarrassing during the meeting," he states as he drops his head.

"How was she when she came home?" asks Jamaal.

Trevon slowly raises his head, shaking it from side to side as he hesitantly says, "Well, I could tell that she was high, but she was okay. However, I'm surprised that she took the time to sit down and talk."

"Yes, that's great! But how could you tell that she was high?" asks Jamaal, his curiosity getting the best of him.

Trevon immediately replies with conviction, "Oh, trust me! I can tell. Her speech is often slurred, and she doesn't look you in the eye. She also tends to be very restless and impatient when she's high. But last night was a little different. I don't know what it was, but her behavior was different. She seemed rather calm. With Mom, you never know what to expect. If she is in a bad mood and we come in the house, she yells. If we try to ask her a question or get too close to her, she pushes us away."

Jamaal cannot imagine what it must be like for Trevon and his siblings to live under the same roof with a person who has a long-standing drug addiction. He is amazed that Trevon has made it as far as he has in life without getting locked up or getting killed. He desperately wants to help Trevon's mother get off drugs so that she can be a real mother to Trevon and his siblings.

He anxiously concludes, "Trevon, man, your mother needs help, and we need to get her the help she needs fast. We're going to be working very hard to get her the help she needs. However, I must say that it doesn't hurt to pray."

Trevon smiles as he thinks about Jamaal's strong faith and belief in God.

"My mother is a strong believer in the power of prayer, and I'm a witness to the fact that God answers prayers. He answered my mom's prayer when she was having a hard time with me. To look at us now, no one would ever know that we've had our fair share of major ups and downs ... and then some."

"Yeah Jamaal, you *are* truly blessed. I have to admit that I've always admired you and your mother. And to be quite honest, I've begun to look at you and your mom as my family," says Trevon with a nervous laugh.

"Well, that's good to hear, because you've always been like a brother to me," Jamaal replies with a warm smile. "You're like the brother I've always wished I had."

"Thanks, man. I needed to hear that," insists Trevon with a wide grin. He looks up at the ceiling pensively and thinks about how blessed he is to have Jamaal as a true friend and confidant.

Jamaal can sense that Trevon is about to say something important, so he remains silent.

Trevon turns to Jamaal and asks, "Hey, Jamaal, you remember back in school when I introduced you to the crew?"

With raised eyebrows, and wondering what is coming, Jamaal cautiously replies, "Yeah."

Trevon discloses, "Well, I never told you, but I was so glad that you decided not to follow through with the initiation process."

Jamaal is not sure where Trevon is going with this comment. He breathes a sigh of relief and continues to give Trevon his undivided attention.

"Man, dealing drugs is no way to go," Trevon states with conviction as he looks Jamaal in the eyes. "Even if you had decided to go through with it, I would have talked you out of it."

"For real?" Jamaal exclaims in disbelief.

Trevon shakes his head from side to side as he thinks about Jamaal's innocent nature. "I could tell that you were smart and had a lot of potential, and I knew that I couldn't allow you to ruin your life by dealing drugs. Man, dealing drugs is no way to live your life. The money is good, for sure, but the risk of losing one's life is not worth it! Man, it's definitely *not* worth it! If I had it to do all over again, I would choose a different path."

Jamaal reflects on how amazing it is that Trevon has survived the streets for so long without getting arrested or killed. His curiosity gets the better of him, and so he musters up the courage to ask, "Trevon, I know that you've been hustling since you were around my age, but I'm curious to know how you kept from getting locked up."

Trevon leans his head back as he lets out a long sigh of frustration. "Jamaal, man, as I think about my life and dealing drugs, I have thoughts about my mother that I would prefer not to be having right now." Trevon can feel himself getting upset as he thinks about his family. He impulsively blurts out, "Not to mention my father—whoever he is or is supposed to be!"

Jamaal can tell that Trevon is getting worked up, and he is afraid that he might end up canceling the family meeting. "Okay, okay!" he interjects. "We won't go there right now. I understand—Trevon, man. I truly do understand."

"Jamaal, you know the deal. Hustling was the only way out that I could come up with at the time. I had no one or nothing else to turn to. But I thank God that our paths crossed, and I thank God for you. I also thank God for allowing me to see that there is still hope for me and my brothers and sister."

Jamaal is relieved to hear Trevon refer to his hope to get help as he announces, "Hey, man, don't forget that there is still hope for your mother, as well."

Trevon cynically replies, "Oh yeah, and Mom too."

Jamaal wonders whether Trevon was able to make contact with his mother's longtime friend. "Did you talk to Ms. Lauren?" he asks.

"Yeah, I stopped by her house on yesterday. She agreed to come tomorrow. She'll meet us at the house at around eleven-thirty. She seemed to be excited about helping Mom, and believe it or not, she asked why I hadn't stopped by earlier."

Jamaal is very pleased that things are coming together as planned. "Seems like everything is set," he enthusiastically declares. "Mom is looking forward to meeting with your mother, and my grandmother will be coming along with us for support."

"Jamaal, I really appreciate all that you and your family have done for me," Trevon sincerely states as he places his hand on Jamaal's shoulder. "It sure feels good to know that someone cares."

Jamaal pats the top of Trevon's hand while emphatically stating, "You bet!"

Trevon looks away from Jamaal and rests his chin in the palm of his hand while reflecting on how fortunate he is to have a friend like Jamaal. "Jamaal, as you know, I'm not very religious, but I do feel blessed. And I thank God for placing you and your mother in my life." He then turns to Jamaal, smiles, and confidently says, "Who knows, I may even get you to teach me how to pray. I know praying is something you do a lot."

Jamaal is surprised that Trevon views him as someone who prays a lot. He replies, "Uh-uh, believe it or not, but I'm just learning how to pray myself. However, I do make it a point to pray each night before I go to bed. That's something that I learned from my grandfather. He would always say his prayers at night before he went to bed."

"Man, you strike me as a person who prays *all the time,*" Trevon states with a smile.

"I go to church and all, and I must admit that I love the Lord … but praying is something that I'm just really learning how to do."

"Man, you may not realize it, but every time I'm around you, it seems like you're praying and thanking God for something or somebody."

"Yes, I pray every night before I go to bed, and I say my grace before I eat. But I don't consider myself to be someone who prays a lot." Jamaal seeks to clarify his faith as he firmly asserts, "Now, I do believe in being prayerful, and I'm constantly asking God to search my heart and help me to be a better person. Truth be told, I'm just beginning to understand what it means to *really* pray. You know, what church folk refer to as *praying with power.*" Jamaal smiles as he thinks about his church family and how serious they become when it's time to pray. He then begins to think about how nice it would be to have someone his age to pray with on a regular basis. He looks Trevon squarely in the eyes and suggests, "If you'd like, we can work on learning how to pray together."

"Hey, I would like that. I could sure use some power in my life! Man, I've tried everything else. Maybe it's time I tried God."

"Great!" Jamaal pronounces with a smile. "I could sure use a prayer partner."

Trevon begins to think about Sunday's service as he looks up at Jamaal. "Oh yeah, I forgot to tell you about what happened in church on Sunday."

"Say what?" Jamaal is taken aback by Trevon's comment. He is very curious to know what he is referring to. "No, you didn't tell me. So, what happened on Sunday?"

"Jamaal, man, you're not going to believe it, but I thought about joining your church when I was there," Trevon confides.

"You know when the preacher was calling for people to come up to join the church? I *seriously* thought about joining."

"Trevon, man, really! Why didn't you tell me?"

Trevon smiles as he replies, "I really wanted to go up, and I was about to mention it to you. But then I began to think about my brothers and sister and how I didn't want to join without them."

"Nah, man, if you had joined, I'm sure they would have been right behind you. Trevon, man, it would be *so cool* to have you join our church. You and your family can join us for service this Sunday. We can see how our family meeting with your mother goes tomorrow. If all goes well, you can all come to church with us this coming Sunday."

"Yeah, that would be nice," Trevon agrees. He thinks about how nice it would be to have his entire family attend church with Jamaal and his mother.

Jamaal is very excited about Trevon's interest in prayer, and he can't believe that Trevon didn't say anything about his interest in joining church last Sunday. Jamaal wants to make it clear to Trevon that he will support his decision to join the church. He swiftly turns to Trevon and looks him squarely in the eyes as he firmly asserts, "Trevon, should you decide that you still want to join our church, *please* let me know. I'd be more than happy to walk down the aisle with you, if you'd like. Okay?"

Trevon shrugs his shoulders as he cheerfully replies, "Cool! That sounds good to me."

Jamaal refocuses their attention on prayer. "For now, we can work on learning how to pray. You know I do believe in the power of prayer, and I know firsthand that prayer changes things." Jamaal smiles as he looks at Trevon and warmly states, "And prayer changes people, as well."

"Yeah, I know. I just wish I had the kind of faith that you have."

"Hey, you never know. You probably have a deeper level of faith than me but just don't know it."

Trevon brushes Jamaal off. "Man, get out of here! I know that that's not so."

"No, Trevon. I'm serious; you never know. For real—I mean it! You've already accepted Christ in your heart, and I have no doubt that God can easily develop your faith to the point where your level of trust and belief in God exceeds mine." Jamaal takes his faith seriously, and he is convinced that a person's faith can easily be developed by accepting Christ as personal Lord and Savior, praying daily, and reading and studying the Word of God. He thinks about how God has developed his faith as he passionately proclaims, "Trevon, man, that's just how good God is!"

Trevon shakes his head from side to side in disbelief, remaining silent as he stares at Jamaal.

"God knows the desires of our hearts. And if you wish to have your faith developed, all you need do is ask God. He'll give you the desires of your heart," Jamaal vehemently declares. "He did it for me, and I'm sure that He will do the same for you, and more!" Jamaal lets out a calming sigh. "I'm not going to press the issue. For now, we can focus on learning how to pray together." Jamaal extends his hands to Trevon while asking, "Are you ready?"

Trevon casually takes Jamaal's hands, saying, "About as ready as I'll ever be."

"Okay. We can start by saying the Lord's Prayer and then add on whatever we would like God to know about us and our circumstances. We will seek His blessings, guidance, direction, and protection over us and our lives, in spirit and truth."

"Okay, that sounds easy enough to me."

Jamaal clasps hands with Trevon, takes on a posture of prayer, and reverently says, "Okay, here we go. We will start with the prayer that Jesus taught his disciples and go from there." Jamaal takes the lead with the Lord's Prayer, and Trevon joins in.

They pray together: "Dear God, You truly are our Father, which art in Heaven. Hollowed be Thy Name. Thy Kingdom come; Thy Will be done on earth as it is in Heaven. We thank you, Father God, for giving us this day our daily bread. Forgive us our trespasses, as we forgive those who trespass against us. Lead us not into temptation, but deliver us from all manner of evil. For Thine is the kingdom, the power, and the glory, forever and ever."

Trevon pauses as Jamaal continues in prayer.

"Dear Heavenly Father, we know that You know what we stand in need of. For You are Lord and Savior of both of our lives, and we truly do love You, worship You, honor You, and adore You. For there is none like You. And I thank You for allowing me and Trevon to become such close friends. Dear God, I pray that You will continue to bless Trevon and his family in a great and mighty way. For we know that You know the thoughts that You think toward us, thoughts of good and not of evil, to give us a future and a hope, and we thank you for that future and that hope. We thank You, Lord God, for Your lovingkindness toward us. For we know that your love toward us will never fail." Jamaal pauses, and Trevon takes over.

"Yes, Lord, we do love You, and I thank You for saving my life. For I know that if it had not been for You, Lord, on my side, I would have been dead and gone a long time ago! Lord, I'm tired of hustling, and I'm tired of watching my mother ruin her life by doing drugs. Lord, I need my mother. She's the only mother that I've got. I don't know what I would do without her. Jamaal has helped me to see that there is hope. And, Father God, it is my earnest plea that You will deliver me and my mother both from drugs." Trevon begins to weep as he cries out to God, "Lord, I don't know what else to do! You and Jamaal are all I have."

CHAPTER 9

FOOLISH PRIDE

Jamaal's father, James, desperately wishes to make contact with his son. However, his fear of being rejected by the woman he still loves dearly is preventing him from picking up the phone to call. James and Marlene have been divorced for eight years, and they have not spoken in over four years. Shortly after the divorce, James was forced to confront his internal struggles related to being adopted as a child and not having a father whom he could turn to for support and guidance. He was able to commit to marriage, and he absolutely loved being a husband. However, following the birth of his son, James's relationship with his wife seemed to change drastically. There was little to no communication between him and Marlene, which caused a strain on their relationship that ultimately led to divorce. James loved Marlene dearly; however, he never would have guessed that having a child would cause his world to come crashing down, slowly but surely.

James knows that he can no longer run from himself. And he is prepared to face his fears around making contact with his ex-wife and their now twelve-year-old son. He is ready to face the reality of what it means to be a true father to his son, and he is determined to conquer the fears that caused him to give up on his marriage and abandon his son in the process. James has decided that he can't let another day go by without contacting his son, so he picks up the phone. He lets out a deep sigh while softly telling himself, "I have to make the call." He nervously dials Marlene's number.

Marlene and Jamaal are in the family room, excitedly talking about how well things are going with Trevon and his family, when the phone rings. They are especially happy about the fact that Trevon's mother joined them for church on Sunday.

Hearing the phone ring, Marlene turns to Jamaal and says, "I'll get it."

Jamaal leaps up from the couch and heads outside to ride his bike.

Marlene is in a very good mood as she answers the phone with great excitement. "Hello!"

James was not sure who would answer the phone and begins to feel butterflies in his stomach at the sound of his ex-wife's voice. He holds the phone to his ear but is unable to speak.

"Hello," Marlene repeats, waiting for a reply. There is no response. She repeats, "Hello? Is anyone there? Hello?"

James badly wishes to speak with Marlene, but his nerves seem to be getting the better of him. He wishes that he could just hang up the phone and pretend that he'd never called.

Marlene again asks, "Hello? Is anyone there?" She patiently waits to see if there is a response.

She begins to move the phone away from her ear when James hesitantly says, "Hello." He then faintly calls out, "Marlene."

Marlene can barely hear James's voice. She intuitively suspects that it is her ex-husband on the other line. She is in a state of disbelief, as she presses the phone to her ear and calmly states, "Hello. James, is that you?"

James remains silent, not knowing what to say or how to respond.

Given the long silence, Marlene is convinced that it is James on the other end. She finds it difficult to contain her emotions. Then she begins to express her feelings, barely taking breaths between sentences. "James, I can't believe it!" she passionately exclaims. "Where in the world have you been? We have not heard from you in over four years. I was beginning to think that something had happened to you. Nobody has heard from you in all this time. For all we knew, you could have been dead!" she angrily cries out.

James tries hard not to let his fears get in the way as he musters up the strength to respond. He takes a deep breath and softly comments, "Marlene, I know, and I deeply apologize. You know that I don't believe in making excuses, so I'm going to be as honest with you as I possibly can. I will try to explain this to you in the best way I know how." James allows his vulnerability to show as he pleads with Marlene. "It was not easy for me to call," he tells her, "but please hear me out."

Marlene shakes her head from side to side in utter disbelief. She lets out a sigh to calm herself and says, "Okay, James, I'm listening," as she prepares to give her ex-husband her undivided attention.

James has made up his mind to be totally honest with Marlene. While not knowing what the outcome will be, he is hoping for the best. He wants a relationship with his son, and he is willing to go through whatever it takes to accomplish that goal, even if it means swallowing his pride. James is humbled by his strength in making contact with his ex-wife. He lets out a calming sigh as he attempts to explain himself. "Well, as you know, when we got married we were both just finishing college. It was clear that you were a very strong woman, and that's what I loved most about you. However, I didn't realize just how strong you were."

Marlene is baffled by James's comment, and she interjects,

"James, I'm not quite sure where you're going with this. I don't quite understand what you mean, but I'm listening."

"As we both know, there was a breakdown in communication, and I totally accept responsibility for my role. And I know that that is something we could have worked through. However, when we stopped spending time together as a couple, I really began to question my role as a husband. You were my best friend, and I knew that I was losing you. And I did not want to hurt you any more than I already had, so I began to pull away."

Marlene begins to feel vulnerable as she listens to James sharing his feelings. His honesty is what she loves most about him. She thinks about how he has never lied to her for as long as they have known each other. Touched by his openness, Marlene shares her feelings too. "Yeah, I know. And as you began to pull away, I began to shut down emotionally. We hardly spoke, and when we did talk it seemed as though we would quickly begin to argue over nothing."

James wishes that he could reach out and embrace Marlene, as he responds, "Marlene, I must say that I never stopped loving you. And I have often wondered deep down in my heart what caused two people who were so much in love to become total strangers almost overnight."

"James, I appreciate your honesty. But I wish we had been able to talk about this before things got out of hand."

"Yeah, I know, and I agree. I thank you for taking the time to listen." James knows that it will take some doing, if they are to work on their relationship. So he decides to shift the focus to his son, Jamaal. "Marlene, there is so much that I would like to share with you, and I know that I also have a lot of explaining to do with my son. However, I can honestly say that I never stopped loving you or him." James is overwhelmed by the love that he still has in his heart for his ex-wife and son. He shakes his head from side to side while thinking to himself, *God knows, we should have never divorced*.

Marlene is starting to feel a little conflicted by her love for her ex-husband and the hurt and disappointment that he has caused her and their son by failing to keep in touch. "But James, I don't understand why you chose not to call," she sternly states. "I wish you had kept in touch. I'm less concerned about myself, but your son has missed you *terribly*! Every time the phone would ring, Jamaal would get excited, hoping that it was you on the other end. You can't begin to imagine what it has been like, trying to protect Jamaal from the anger, hurt, and disappointment that he experienced in not being able to see nor talk with you. You were the most important person in his life. James; he *really* looked up to you."

James is moved by Marlene's deep sense of love and compassion for their son, and he humbly replies, "Yeah, I know, and believe me, I do plan to try my best to make up for all the hurt and pain that I've caused him over the years. I just hope it's not too late." James pauses as he recalls how difficult it was for him to pick up the phone to call this time. "Marlene, I thought about calling many times, but I just could not bring myself to call before knowing that I had gotten my own life back on track. I loved being a husband. I also loved being a provider and being able to take care of you. However, after Jamaal was born, I quickly began to feel like an outsider looking in. I felt like I had lost my place in your heart, and I didn't know where to start in trying to be a father to our son."

Marlene's mood softens as she begins to reflect on her love for James and the fact that he is the only man that she has ever truly loved. "James, I'm listening, and I hope you know that I never stopped loving you. My feelings for you have not changed. Please know that I will always have a special place in my heart for you."

James begins to smile inwardly as he continues to confide his feelings. "Marlene, to be honest, I didn't feel that I was good enough for you. I always felt like you deserved better. However, I was determined to prove that I was worthy of your love, so I began to focus on working fifty to sixty hours a week. I still ended up with a paycheck that was far less than yours. Not only was I coming up short as a provider, I didn't have a clue about how to be a father." James pauses as he thinks about how perfect Marlene seemed to be in all she did, especially when it came to taking care of Jamaal. "Marlene, you were such a perfect mother. It seemed like motherhood came naturally for you."

Marlene is listening intently to James. Her emotions begin to come through as she passionately states, "James, I *love* being a mother, but I also *loved* being a wife. When we married, I *never* imagined I would be one to get a divorce. We were so right for each other. You helped me to balance my life. And I *never*, in my wildest dreams, thought that we would end up getting a divorce."

"Me neither," James calmly states. "But compared to you, I just seemed to be so flawed. I began to feel that I could not do anything right. Then I began to notice how much you loved our son and how gentle you were with him. It seemed *so* perfect. It seemed like you didn't have a care in the world, and little Jamaal seemed like he was the happiest child on earth. As I watched you with Jamaal, I got to the point where I convinced myself that you and Jamaal were better off without me. I felt like I was more of a burden than a help to you."

Marlene is caught off guard by James's comments. "Oh, James, that was not so!" she exclaims. She pauses to collect her thoughts. "I wish you had said something. You know that you could talk to me about anything, and I do mean *anything*. Is that not true?"

"Marlene, I know, but I didn't want you to feel sorry for me or pity me. That would have only made things worse. I ran away because I was confused and scared. To tell the truth, I have been running from myself ever since the divorce. God knows I would have never left you or our baby boy if I had been thinking straight."

Marlene knows James very well and understands his feelings. She softly replies, "Yes, I know."

"Marlene, I now realize that I never should have let so much time pass without being in touch with the two of you."

"No, James, you should *not* have. But I am beginning to understand a little better why you chose not to make contact with us." Still, reflecting on all that she and Jamaal have been through over the past four years, Marlene tells him, "I do understand why you found it difficult to make contact, but I don't condone it. Nevertheless, I appreciate your being very open and honest with me. And I do look forward to your being able to speak with your son."

"Thanks, Marlene, and yes, I'm really looking forward to seeing and speaking with Jamaal." James is grateful for Marlene's willingness to listen and hear him out.

Marlene smiles as she thinks about how Jamaal has grown and matured over the past four years. "Yes, he's a very bright child, and I know that you will be very proud of him. He's also quite good at speaking his mind." Marlene's smile broadens as she thinks about how outspoken their son is. She has no doubt that Jamaal will share his true feelings with his father without holding back. "I will let Jamaal fill you in on what has been going on in his life. I'm sure that he will be able to fill you in on all that he has been going through for the past four years."

James is very excited about making contact with Jamaal; however, he is concerned about how Jamaal will respond to him. He presses his ear against the phone, remaining silent, as he listens intently to every word that Marlene says.

Marlene suspects that James is concerned about being rejected by Jamaal, so she tries to calm his fears by lightening the mood. "James, please know that you have nothing to worry about. Jamaal loves you dearly, and I'm quite sure that he would love to hear from you. All that boy ever talks about is his daddy. She lightheartedly begins to mimic Jamaal: 'When am I going to hear from my daddy?' 'Where's my daddy?' 'Will I ever get to see my dad again?' 'Why doesn't Daddy call?'" Marlene lets out a long sigh as she emphatically states in a sarcastic tone, "I may be highly intelligent, but those were questions I could not answer."

James inwardly smiles as he warmly replies, "Yes, I know, and I do apologize."

"James, Jamaal was beginning to think that you didn't love him or care about him," Marlene discloses, her mood becoming more serious. "He took your not calling to mean that you didn't have an interest in him. I tried to reassure him that you loved him dearly, hoping deep down that you would call one day." Marlene takes a deep breath and shakes her head. "James, I honestly don't know how to say this, but you cannot begin to imagine all that I have been through trying to cover for you these past four years."

James's mood becomes solemn as he thinks about the pain that he has caused his ex-wife and son. "Please accept my sincere apology. Marlene, I know that you have done an excellent job in raising our son, and I thank you," he states in an attempt to shift the mood and focus of the conversation. "I never doubted your strength nor your ability to raise our son. I just regret that I was not around to help. Yes, I regret that I have not been the father that Jamaal deserves. I have missed eight years of raising my son, and yes, I do look forward to spending quality time with him."

"Oh, I have no doubt that he will be very excited to hear from you," Marlene asserts. "You know, James, I had almost given up hope of ever hearing from you, but I'm very glad that you found the courage to call. I know that Jamaal will be very surprised to hear from you. I also know that he will be quick to forgive you and forget that you have been out of his life for as long as you have. I just hope you are able to promise yourself that you will never lose contact with him again."

"Marlene, before picking up the phone, I prayed that you would receive my call and not hang up on me. I have been praying about how to go about reconnecting with you and our son for a long time. I also told myself that if you took the time to hear me out and gave me a second chance at reconnecting with my son, I would never lose contact with you or him ever again."

Marlene is deeply moved by James's comment and takes a deep breath as tears begin to well up in her eyes. "Well, that's good. James, that is *so good* to hear."

"Marlene, I know that I don't deserve a second chance with you, or our son for that matter, but I thank you for taking the time to hear me out. You were, and still are, my one and only true best friend, and I pray that that will never change."

Marlene tries not to let James know that his honesty has moved her to tears as she responds, "Well, since we're being honest, I must say that Jamaal is not the only one who has missed you. I have to admit that I never stopped loving you. And yes, you are still, and will always be, my very best friend."

James knows Marlene well and can sense that she has been weeping silently on the other end of the phone. Tears begin to form in his eyes, as well, as he sits silently on the other end of the phone, fighting them back.

Marlene pauses as she regains her composure and then breaks the silence. "James, I know that we have been divorced for almost eight years and have not spoken with each other in over four years. However, when God placed you in my life, I knew that there was something very special about you, and I have not let go of that."

The open and honest manner in which Marlene expresses herself is what James loves most about her. He begins to think about how his love for her has remained as strong as it was when they first married. "Marlene, you are one very special lady, and I don't know how I survived these past eight years without you. I have really missed you. I wanted to call you a long time ago, but I was too afraid."

Marlene replies, "James, you know I love you and I would never outright reject you. I am *so glad* that you took the chance in calling." Marlene pauses as she shakes her head from side to side. She is thinking about how well they used to communicate with each other.

James is relieved by Marlene's expression of love and acceptance, as he lovingly replies, "Yes, Marlene. I am too."

Marlene sighs. "James, I think that we have all suffered long enough. I truly do thank God for our new beginning. Welcome home, and trust me when I say that you have always been a wonderful husband and it is never too late to learn how to be a good father. The good thing about it is that you now have a twelve-year-old son to help you out along the way." Marlene chuckles as she thinks again about how outspoken Jamaal can be. "I have no doubt that your son will gladly give you feedback on how you're doing as a father, and he will definitely let you know when you're 'just not getting it.' Trust me, I know from experience."

James takes a deep breath as he reflects on all that has been shared between them. "Marlene, I tell you, it's so good to be able to smile again." The smile on his face broadens.

"Yes, and I'm sure that you will be doing a lot of smiling, laughing, and maybe even shedding a few tears as you and Jamaal begin to spend more and more time together." Marlene smiles as she reflects on her role as mother *and* father to Jamaal. "Our son has definitely taught me a thing or two about being a mother, and I'm glad that you are willing to step back into his life as a father."

"I consider your accepting me back into your life and giving me a second chance with our son a true blessing. I have always believed in miracles, but I now know that miracles do come true. I never imagined that our conversation would go so smoothly, and I do thank God for you and pray that He will allow us to continue to work on putting the pieces back together again."

Marlene smiles as she listens to James. She notices how much he has grown spiritually over the past four years, and she decides to invite him to attend church with her and Jamaal. "James, I know that you are looking forward to seeing Jamaal. I'd like to invite you to join us for church on Sunday. After church, you and Jamaal can spend the balance of the day together."

James's eyes widen as the thought of seeing his ex-wife and son floods his mind. He did not think that an offer would be made for him to see them so soon. "Marlene, I would *love* that," he tells her enthusiastically.

"That's great! We can let it be a surprise for Jamaal. I won't tell him about our conversation, and Sunday you can come by to pick us up. I know Jamaal would love that. He's going to be so surprised to see you."

"I thank you, Marlene," says James with deep sincerity. "I am truly looking forward to seeing you and Jamaal on Sunday. Please know that I do love you and our son dearly."

"Yes, I know," Marlene softly replies with a smile. "Good night, James," she says as she prepares to hang up the phone.

"Good night Marlene, and thank you again for everything."

"You're welcome, James. Jamaal and I will see you on Sunday." Marlene smiles as she hangs up the phone. Then she leans back on the couch and closes her eyes as she contemplates her undying love for James. It almost seems as if they'd never separated. She then begins to ponder how the thought of remarrying anyone besides James has never entered her mind. She feels convinced that she and James are meant to get back together; their phone conversation seemed so perfect. Before going to bed, Marlene offers a prayer of thanksgiving for her family.

"Dear God, You know that I love my husband dearly, and I thank You for bringing him back into my life. Lord, You know that I have often thought about what it would be like to have James back in my life and in his son's life. However, I never imagined that I would see this day come true. Dear God, You know what is best for me and my son, as well as my ex-husband, and I thank You for seeing fit to have us reconnect in the manner in which You have allowed us to. Lord, I pray that Jamaal will be open to receiving his father back into his life, in spite of all the hurt and pain that he has been through. I know that James means well and desires to be the best father that he is able to be to our son. Lord, I also know that he has only desired what he felt was best for me as a wife as well as a mother."

Marlene pauses as she thinks about her love for her son and ex-husband, and then she continues to pray: "Heavenly Father, I place all things in Your hands right now, knowing that we have not made the best decisions over the past several years. I pray, dear God, that You will forgive each of us for our sins. For all have sinned and fall short of Your Glory. Thank You, Lord, for giving my son a second chance at getting to know his father. Lord, I do not know why we were separated for as long as we have been. However, I know that You know all things, and I will not question Your sovereignty. Lord, I place my faith and trust in You, praying that You will have Your way in our lives. I pray that we will keep You first in all that we do. I love You, Lord. And I thank You for all that You have done, are doing, and plan to do in my life and in the life of my family, now and forevermore. In Jesus's name I pray. Amen."

CHAPTER 10

MENDING THE BROKEN PIECES

Sunday morning, Marlene is in the kitchen, preparing breakfast, as Jamaal races downstairs and scurries in.

"Well, good morning," Marlene cheerfully expresses as she turns to give Jamaal a warm hug. "How's my favorite son?" she lightheartedly asks.

Jamaal has a big grin on his face. "Mom, I feel great!" he excitedly exclaims. "For some reason, I feel great, and I'm really looking forward to going to church this morning,"

Surprised by Jamaal's level of excitement over attending church, Marlene jokingly asks, "Might it possibly be that you're excited about being the only male in your Sunday school class?"

Jamaal brushes his mother off as he chuckles under his breath. "Oh, Mom, you know that I'm not interested in any of those girls. I don't have time to be thinking about girls right now. My focus is on getting my grades up so that I can get accepted into the Duke Ellington School of the Arts." Jamaal pauses as he thinks about what it would be like to become a famous actor and movie director. He is extremely gifted in science, technology, and mathematics; however, he has always had an interest in acting and would like to one day own his own movie production company. While thinking about his hopes and dreams for the future, Jamaal begins to think about Trevon. He seeks to gain his mother's attention. "Mom," he softly calls as he turns and looks in her direction while reaching for the refrigerator door.

"Yes, dear," Marlene replies. She can sense that Jamaal has something important to say, so she places the dish towel on the counter and takes a seat at the kitchen table.

Jamaal grabs a carton of juice out of the refrigerator. He walks over to the table where his mother is seated, pulls up a chair next to her, and enthusiastically asks, "Did I tell you about Trevon's interest in music? He wants to be a music producer. He's also interested in having his own recording studio." He blurts this excitedly as he fills his glass with juice.

"Jamaal, sweetheart, that is absolutely wonderful. And he seems to be doing really well in school." Marlene smiles as she thinks about how very proud she is of her son and his friend Trevon. "Trevon's mother told me that they are thinking about promoting him to the ninth grade. If he attends summer school, he'll be placed in his correct grade the following year. And son, if I haven't told you lately, I would like you to know that I'm *very proud* of both you and Trevon. You are both doing so well in school."

Jamaal remains silent, but the smile on his face broadens as he thinks about how well Trevon is doing in school.

"I'm also very proud of Trevon's mother for sticking with the rehab program." Marlene thinks about how she was able to get Trevon's mother to enroll in the residential drug treatment program. She has done this by helping her realize how much she means to her children and how badly they need her to be active in their lives.

"Trevon is very excited about the progress that his mother is making!" exclaims Jamaal.

"Yes, dear, Trevon's mother is doing an outstanding job in reclaiming her life. She is slowly learning to truly love and forgive herself while simultaneously taking a genuine interest in her children. As a matter of fact, I will be attending an upcoming awards dinner, where she will be recognized for successfully completing the first phase of the program."

"Mom, I'm so glad that you were able to help Trevon's mother. And, it's great that you will be attending the awards dinner with her next week."

"Yes, I'm glad that she selected me to be one of her invited guests, and I am truly looking forward to being there." Marlene leans down and gently kisses Jamaal on the forehead. She is amazed by the progress that Trevon and his family have made over the past six months. Knowing how difficult it has been on Jamaal not having his father play an active role in his life, Marlene cannot begin to image how Trevon and his siblings made it this far in life without having either parent actively involved in their lives. God knows it was nothing short of a miracle. *Those adorable kids desperately needed their mother,* Marlene thinks to herself as she silently thanked God that Trevon's mother was sticking with the drug treatment program.

Jamaal begins to think about how well Trevon is doing in school. He looks up at his mother and tells her excitedly, "Momma, I'm so glad that Trevon is really focused on his academics now! He is making As and Bs in all of his classes, which is unbelievable! I always knew that he was smart, but I didn't think that he would be *that* interested in school. He also seems to be getting along really well with his teachers." Jamaal chuckles as he looks up at his mother and jokingly declares, "Trevon almost seems to be more excited about graduating high school than I am."

Marlene smiles as she shakes her head from side to side. She prayerfully reflects on how much her son means to her, while lovingly wondering, *Lord, what am I going to do with this little one here? He is constantly reminding me of why I love him so much.*

Jamaal smiles as he says, "I'm going to really miss seeing Trevon around school next year, but I know that we'll keep in touch." His eyes widen as he recalls his inspiring conversation with Trevon. "Oh, Mom, I forgot to tell you—Trevon and I are planning on going into business together. We want to own our own production company." Jamaal briefly pauses as a thought crosses his mind. "Hey, I just came up with a name!" he enthusiastically exclaims. "We can call our production company JT Productions and Associates." He laughs as he looks up at his mother and states with conviction, "We can have Trevon's old crew work for us. That way we can help others and give back to the community."

"Son, that would be wonderful," Marlene assures him as she places her hand on his shoulder. "And as you know, I'll be standing behind the two of you one hundred percent; and that's a promise," she firmly declares.

"Thanks, Mom!" Jamaal leans over and gives his mother a great big hug. He is in an unusually good mood, although he doesn't know why. He calmly turns and looks at Marlene, telling her, "Mom, it's kind of weird, but I feel especially good this morning. For some reason, I feel that this is going to be the *best day* of my life."

Marlene is somewhat stunned by her son's comment. He doesn't yet know that his father is coming to pick them up for church. "Well, son, that's good to hear," Marlene asserts. "All I can say is that God truly is good, and I'm looking forward to attending church as well," she adds.

"Oh, Mom, you're always looking forward to going to church. You *love* church!" Jamaal lets out a hearty laugh as he thinks about how much time his mother spends at church, attending church ministry meetings, Sunday school, and Bible study. He chuckles while confessing, "I love church too, but I'm *so glad* that I'm not a preacher's kid."

"Now, why would you say that? And, what do you know about being a preacher's kid?" Marlene playfully asks.

"Not much," Jamaal admits. "But being a preacher's kid doesn't seem like it would be much fun." He laughs under his breath, looks up at his mother and smiles, as he asks playfully, not expecting an answer, "Who would want to be in church all the time? I would guess that a preacher's kid would end up being in church at least three to four times a week and *all day* on Sundays!"

Marlene begins to playfully wrestle and tickle Jamaal, joking around. "Yes, and what, might I ask, is wrong with that?"

The phone rings as Jamaal is about to respond.

Marlene suspects that it is Jamaal's father calling, so she casually states, "I'd better grab that. You never know who might be calling."

Jamaal finishes his breakfast as his mother goes into the den to answer the phone. Marlene answers the phone with a lively voice. "Hello."

"Hello, Marlene," James responds. "I just wanted to call to let you know that I'm on my way. I'll be stopping to get gas, and I'll give you a call when I get close to your house."

Marlene is pleased to know that James has not changed his mind. She also thinks about how punctual and considerate he has always been, as she warmly replies, "Okay, thanks. See you shortly." Marlene hangs up the phone and calls out, "Jamaal, sweetheart!"

"Yes ma'am!"

"Are you about ready for church?"

"Just about."

Marlene smiles as she thinks about how surprised Jamaal

is going to be to see his father. "Okay, our ride should be here shortly.

"Okay. Who's picking us up?" Jamaal enthusiastically asks.

"It's a surprise," Marlene coyly states. "You'll find out soon enough."

Jamaal smiles as he asserts, "Oh, I know. It's Grandma." He seeks confirmation from his mother. "Grandma's coming to pick us up for church, right?"

Marlene smiles as she looks up at the ceiling while smugly answering, "I'm not saying; you'll find out soon enough."

Jamaal is convinced that it is his grandmother, but he does wonder why his mom would want it be a surprise. He goes into the den to grab his jacket, as he prepares to head out the side door to wait on his grandmother. "You can't fool me," Jamaal confidently asserts. "I know it is Grandma. Who else would be coming to pick us up?" He joyfully heads outside.

Marlene is in the kitchen straightening up when the phone rings. She quickly answers. "Hello."

"Marlene, this is James. I wanted to let you know I'm just around the corner."

"Okay, great. Jamaal is in the front yard waiting on you to arrive. However, he has no idea that it will be you picking us up for church. He is going to be quite surprised."

"Thank you, Marlene. It was very sweet of you to allow me to pick you two up. I'll see you shortly."

"You're welcome, James." Marlene hangs up the phone. She opens the side door and calls out to Jamaal. "Jamaal, sweetheart, our ride will be here shortly. I'm going to lock up the house, and I'll be right out."

As James pulls up into the driveway, Jamaal is puzzled by the fact that he does not recognize either the car or the driver. He slowly walks toward the car and leans his head to the side in order to get a glimpse at the driver. *Who could it be?* Jamaal wonders. He cautiously walks to the passenger's side, leans his head inside the open window, and introduces himself. "Hi, I'm Jamaal."

"Yes, I know," James replies.

Jamaal pauses as he stares into the car with an even more puzzled look. "Dad …?" he asks in amazement.

James smiles as he looks at his son's face. His eyes begin to fill with tears as he sees Jamaal's eyes widen in recognition.

Jamaal mumbles under his breath, "No way, I can't believe this." Incredulous and overwhelmed with excitement, he cries out, "Dad!"

"Yes, son!" James enthusiastically replies.

Jamaal swings open the passenger side door and jumps into the front seat. He leans into his father's outstretched arms, as both of them well up with tears. They are so excited to see one another and find it hard to let go of the embrace that seems to warm their hearts. James softly states, "Son, I've truly missed you," as they both fight back the tears.

As Marlene locks the side door, she sees her son and his father talking and laughing inside the car. She cannot believe her eyes. As she looks on, tears roll down her cheeks. She quickly composes herself as she heads out the front door and confidently walks up to the car.

"Mommy, Mommy!" cries Jamaal. "It's Dad! Dad is here!"

"Yes, dear, I know. I know," replies Marlene.

"Oh, Mommy, Daddy is back!" Jamaal exclaims, bursting into tears.

Marlene remains silent as she fights back the tears.

Jamaal regains his composure, wipes his eyes, and turns to his mom. "Thank you for giving me such a wonderful surprise. This is the happiest day of my life! I can't wait to tell Trevon about seeing Dad. I didn't think I would ever see this day. I didn't think I would ever see Dad again!"

James chimes in, "Marlene, I thank you too. I thank you for giving me the opportunity to see my son."

Marlene tenderly replies, "You are both very welcome," as she discreetly wipes the tears from her eyes.

James turns to Jamaal and says, "Son, I want you to know that your mother made it possible for me to see you."

Jamaal remains silent, but the smile on his face broadens as he looks at his mother.

James also looks at Marlene, while lovingly stating, "Son, you have one very special mother, and I love both of you very much."

"Yes, Dad, I know." Jamaal then quickly turns to his dad and asks, "But where have you been? I have not seen you in over four years." Jamaal drops his head in sadness as he discloses, "Dad, I really missed you."

"Yes, I know, son. I have missed you too," James replies. "But I'm back, and I plan to fill you in on everything that has been going on with me over the past several years, and that's a promise—"

Marlene interjects. "Yes, son. After church, your dad plans to take you to dinner, and the two of you can spend the rest of the evening getting caught up."

Jamaal perks up, and his eyes widen. He looks up at his dad and excitedly asks, "Can I spend the night?"

James is taken aback by his son's request. He remains silent, wondering if Marlene will allow Jamaal to spend the night.

Jamaal pleads with his mother, crying out, "Please, Mommy, please! Can I *please* spend the night with Daddy?"

Marlene understands Jamaal's excitement; however, she is not sure that spending the night with his father so soon after making contact would be a good idea. "Son, you have to go to school tomorrow, and I'm not sure of your father's schedule. Let's take it one step at a time." Marlene turns to James and looks him firmly in the eyes while she speaks to her son: "Jamaal, sweetheart, your father is back, and I don't think that he plans to leave again anytime soon." Marlene's eyes remain fixed on James as she awaits his reply.

James thinks to himself, *I know that look.* He completely understands Marlene's concern. He turns to Jamaal and states, "Son, your mother's right. I am back. And I don't plan to lose contact with you or your mother ever again. All I really want to do is make up for lost time. And trust me, son, when I say that I want to be the best father I can possibly be for as long as I have breath in my body." James pauses and then firmly states, "I mean that from the depth of my heart."

Jamaal joyfully replies, "Okay! But no amount of time will be too much for me." Jamaal's mood shifts as he thinks about all that he has been through over the past several years. He leans his head to the side, looks up at his dad, and hesitantly states, "Dad, I can't wait to fill you in on everything that has been happening."

"Son, there is so much that I would like to share with you as well," states James with a smile of love and reassurance.

Jamaal smiles as he senses the love that his father has for him. He excitedly exclaims, "Dad, I told Mom this morning that I felt like this was going to be the *best day* of my life, and it truly has been." Having his dad back in his life is like a dream come true.

James looks at his watch as he replies, "But son, the day is just beginning."

Jamaal's smile broadens as he enthusiastically replies, "Yeah, Dad, I know, but it already feels like the best day of my life!"

James laughs as he listens to his son with great love and admiration.

The smile on Marlene's face widens as she listens in on the conversation between her son and his father. "My, my, my! Are we in paradise, or is this heaven?" she playfully asks.

Jamaal quickly replies, "Mom, it feels like heaven to me."

James agrees with his son. "Yes, it sure does. It certainly does."

Marlene smiles and shakes her head from side to side. She is amazed by how perfect the day appears to be going.

James parks the car in front of the church. He leans over to kiss Marlene on the cheek, and he thanks her once again for making this day possible. He then asks, "Are you two ready to head inside?"

Jamaal smiles as he sees how well his parents seem to be getting along. He then begins to wonder what could possibly have caused them to get a divorce. He decides this will be one of the first questions he asks his dad during their special time together. Jamaal calls out to his parents with great excitement, "Mom! Dad!"

James and Marlene simultaneously look at each other and then turn in Jamaal's direction to give him their undivided attention.

With great joy, Jamaal smiles and announces, "It sure feels great to be attending church together as one big happy family!"

James smiles as he gently takes Jamaal by the hand. He thinks about the last time he attended church with his son and ex-wife. To his amazement, he vividly recalls the sermon that was preached from the Book of Proverbs, Chapter 22, and the words of wisdom contained there within.

Marlene takes Jamaal's other hand as they walk toward the church. She thinks about how much she loves her son as she confirms his comment: "Yes, son, it sure does feel good to be attending church as a family, and I want you to know that we both love you very much."

"Son, your mother is right. We both do love you very much," affirms James with great conviction.

Jamaal is filled with glee as he lovingly replies, "Thanks, Dad!

Thanks, Mom! I love you too. I love you both very, very much, and I'm so glad that you're my parents."

James and Marlene simultaneously state, "Son, we are very proud to be your parents." The fact that James and Marlene expressed the same exact thought brings about a hearty laugh as they walk up the steps to the church. They proudly enter as a family to be seated, as the Sunday school class that is held in the sanctuary comes to an end and praise and worship begins, in preparation for the ten o'clock worship service that will follow.

CHAPTER 11

MALE BONDING

It's Sunday morning once again, and Jamaal is excited about attending church with his parents. He rushes to get dressed. Marlene also is looking forward to attending church. However, she has a high-profile court case that she needs to prepare closing arguments for, so she will need to return home immediately afterward. James arrives early to pick them up. Jamaal sees his father pulling up into the driveway. He races outside, hops into the front seat, and buckles his seat belt. He lets his father know that his mother will be driving to church separately. He also tells him that Marlene will not be able to join them for dinner. James expresses his understanding as he prepares to back out of the driveway.

Jamaal, his father, and his mother thoroughly enjoy the church service. Jamaal gives his mother a warm hug as he and his father walk her to her car. James opens Marlene's car door, leans in, and gives her a kiss on the cheek as she prepares to head home.

As Jamaal and his father are walking to his car, Jamaal thinks about how much he values the quality time that he is able to spend with his father while filling him in on all that has been going on in his life. Spending this time with his father is like a dream come true for Jamaal, and it is an experience he now wishes to share with his friend Trevon. Jamaal wants his father to establish a bond with Trevon that is similar to the bond that has developed between the two of them.

"Dad, I'm so glad that you came back," Jamaal tells him for the tenth time as his father prepares to enter the Thurgood Marshall expressway en route to the restaurant. "This is like a dream come true. I was beginning to think that I was never going to see you again," Jamaal solemnly states.

"Son, it's so good to be back," James maintains as he places his hand on Jamaal's shoulder. "I thank your mother, and I also thank you for being so understanding and for accepting me with open arms."

"You are my dad," Jamaal tells him. "And no one will ever take your place." He then begins to think about his friend Trevon and his siblings. "But Dad, I didn't realize how bad I needed you in my life until I started middle school and met my friend Trevon."

James is listening intently to his son as he shares his feelings. He looks over at Jamaal and softy replies, "Oh yeah?" as he continues to listen attentively.

"Trevon is my best friend. He's about to turn sixteen and really needs a man in his life. He needs someone to sit down and talk with him. We talk all the time, but he needs someone like a father to spend time with him." Jamaal pauses as he thinks about the pain that Trevon has been through in not knowing his father and having such an unresponsive mother. "My friend Trevon is really hurting inside, because he doesn't know who his father is, and his mother has not been able to raise him because of her substance abuse. She's doing much better, but she has been addicted to drugs for as long as Trevon can remember."

In listening to his son, James begins to realize how similar Trevon's life experience is to his own, and he sincerely thinks about what his son is saying.

Jamaal looks intently at his dad and asks, "Dad, can you talk with Trevon? He has spent most of his life trying so hard to keep his head up while trying to provide for his younger brothers and sister. Mom has been keeping in touch with Trevon's mother, and his mother is finally getting help for her drug addiction." Jamaal pauses as he drops his head in sadness. "But Dad, Trevon needs a male role model in his life. Someone that he can talk to about all the things that are going on in his life. Someone who he can look up to for guidance and advice."

Jamaal's father begins to feel a deep sense of sadness as he thinks about the years that he has missed spending with Jamaal. He remains attentive.

"I can really relate to Trevon," states Jamaal. He lifts his head and looks in his dad's direction as he continues. "There were times when I felt like giving up and throwing in the towel. Mom and I were constantly arguing, and nothing seemed to be going right. I hated being around Mom, to the point where I thought about running away from home. I just wanted to call it quits! I came close to just giving up on life, until I was able to talk with Grandma. Grandma helped me realize how much she and Mom really love me and care about me. But Dad, nothing compares to having a father."

James realizes that he could have literally lost his son to the streets if Jamaal's grandmother had not intervened. He admires Jamaal's commitment and level of concern for his friend Trevon. James enthusiastically extends an invitation: "Son, I would love to meet Trevon. Maybe he can join us for dinner."

Jamaal is quite surprised by his father's offer, and he joyfully proclaims, "Oh, Dad, that would be great! I know that Trevon would love that! I can call him now to see if he's home."

"Sure." James passes his phone to Jamaal.

"Thanks, Dad," Jamaal says as he dials Trevon's number.

He listens as the phone rings and Trevon answers, "Hello."

"Hey, Trevon, it's me, Jamaal! I'm here with my dad. We wondered if you wanted to join us for dinner," he shouts happily.

"Yeah, sure. I would love to!" Trevon is delightfully amazed by the offer.

"Okay, we'll come get you," states Jamaal enthusiastically.

"Oh, okay," replies Trevon.

Jamaal looks in his father's direction with raised eyebrows and states, "We'll see you in about twenty minutes."

James nods to confirm that twenty minutes is a good estimate without knowing exactly where Trevon lives.

"Okay! I'll be waiting outside," Trevon tells him.

"Okay, we'll see you in a little while." Jamaal can hardly contain his excitement. "Trevon is going to come for dinner. He lives on the corner of Nelson Mandela Boulevard and the new Barack Obama Parkway," he gleefully states as he hands the phone back to his dad.

"Oh, he lives on the south side of town. I know exactly where that is. That's not far from the restaurant that we're going to." Jamaal's father is a native Washingtonian who loves to talk about the history of the District of Columbia. He turns to Jamaal and states, "Son, you know that area of town has a rich history that very few people know about. We're going to have to schedule some time to go sightseeing so that I can fill you in on the history surrounding the area where you and Trevon live."

Jamaal begins to exuberantly bounce up and down in his seat, as he exclaims, "Oh, Dad, that would be great! I'm so glad that Trevon will be joining us for dinner. Maybe he can come on our sightseeing tour of the District of Columbia as well."

"Yes, son, that would be fine, and yes, I'm glad that your friend Trevon will be joining us." As James pulls into Trevon's driveway, he reaches over to give Jamaal a firm hug of love and support.

Jamaal warmly embraces him back.

Trevon notices the car pulling into the driveway and rushes over to greet Jamaal and his father. Jamaal jumps out to meet him while beckoning him to sit in the front. "Hey, Trevon, go ahead; you can sit in the front." Jamaal swings open the door and hops into the back seat, but Trevon remains standing next to the car.

Trevon feels bad about taking Jamaal's seat, but in the end he obliges. He turns to Jamaal's father to greet him. "Good afternoon, Mr. James. I'm Trevon," he states while reaching to buckle his seat belt.

"Yes, son, I know. I'm very pleased to meet you."

"Pleased to meet you as well." Trevon smiles as he looks Jamaal's father in the face and softly states, "Wow, no one has ever called me *son* before."

James remains silent. He has never heard anyone refer to him as *son* either.

Trevon glances in the back seat at Jamaal and decides to speak up. "Mr. James, I really appreciate your coming by to pick me up. I've heard so much about you. Jamaal talks about you all the time. And I do mean all the time!"

"Seeing how close you and my son are, I would love to spend as much time with you as you would like," James firmly insists. "Jamaal tells me that the two of you are like brothers," he adds.

Trevon's eyes widen, as does the smile on his face. "Yes sir," he promptly confirms. "There's a special bond between me and Jamaal. I have a lot of brothers, and I can honestly say that Jamaal and I are a lot *closer* than brothers." Trevon turns to Jamaal and begins to chuckle as he thinks about his relationship with his siblings. "Mr. James, sir, there are days when I envy Jamaal and wish that I was an only child."

Jamaal and his father both chuckle at Trevon's lighthearted comment.

"And thanks, Mr. James, for your offer to spend time with me. I would *love* that," he warmly comments.

"Trevon, I've heard a lot about you and your family. And I must say that you seem like a good kid with a lot of potential."

Jamaal is smiling from ear to ear as he listens in on the conversation between his father and his best friend.

Trevon hesitates. "Well, I know that I have hopes and dreams, but no one has ever encouraged them. Jamaal is the only one who knows anything about my plans for the future, and you are the first adult man to say anything positive about me."

James is saddened by what he is hearing. "Well, I truly feel that my son is lucky to have you as a best friend."

"Thanks, Mr. James," Trevon says happily.

"No, thank *you*," James insists with conviction. "I appreciate your being there for my son and looking out for him. He told me all about what he has gone through over the past couple of years."

"He did?" Trevon is shocked by the fact that Jamaal has told his father all that.

"Yes, son, and he also told me all about how you two first met and what the two of you have been going through over the past year. I know that Jamaal views you as a brother, and if you don't mind, I would love to stand in for your father." James pauses as he clarifies. "That is, until you are able to meet and get to know your true father for yourself."

Jamaal is unable to contain his excitement as he exuberantly yells out, "Oh, Dad, that would be *so cool*!"

Trevon is deeply moved by James's offer. "Thank you, Mr. James. I would love that. I would really love that!"

"Well, boys, we're here," James announces. "I don't know about the two of you, but I'm *starving*."

"Yeah, me too," replies Jamaal.

"Yes, I am too," states Trevon.

"Have you been here before?" asks Jamaal.

"Nah, man, this is my first time." Trevon's mood becomes solemn. He had never been to a formal restaurant prior to meeting Jamaal and his mother.

Jamaal's mood remains upbeat, and he enthusiastically tells his friend, "Oh, you're going to *love it*! They have the best sea-food in town. They also have a video arcade where we can play some of the coolest games while waiting for our food. I discovered these antique video machines where you can play Pac-Man, Ms. Pac-Man, and Galaga—some games that are really challenging and fun."

"Really?" Trevon disbelievingly asks as he looks at Jamaal. He is amazed by his description of the restaurant.

Jamaal nods his head. "Yep, that's right. I'll show you around once we get inside."

James smiles as he walks in behind his son and Trevon. "Hey, remember that we need to order our food before you guys head off to the game room," he reminds them. "That is, if you're interested in eating!" he jokingly adds.

James thoroughly enjoys dining out with Jamaal and Trevon. After finishing dinner, the boys spend more time playing video games. James remains seated at the table, where he reflects on what it means to be a father to his son and a surrogate father to his son's best friend. This causes him to think about how much he has missed by failing to keep in touch with Jamaal and Marlene. He had not realized how profoundly his absence would affect his son. And he'd never imagined that his mere presence could mean so much to a young person whom he hardly knew. Now that he is back in his son's life, and seeing how close Jamaal and Trevon have become, James makes up his mind to remain actively in-volved in both their lives for as long as he is alive and well.

After dropping Trevon and Jamaal off at their homes, James

begins to fantasize about how things could have been had he and Marlene remained married. But he puts the thought out of his mind as he heads home to catch the tail end of the NFL playoff game between the Washington "Burgundy and Gold" team and the Baltimore Ravens.

CHAPTER 12

REUNITED IN LOVE

A year has passed, and James's focus has been on establishing a bond with his son. However, over the past several months he has been thinking more and more about Marlene and what it would be like if they were to remarry. James has wanted to make sure he had given his son his undivided attention, making up for lost time, before asking his ex-wife out on a date. Jamaal, on the other hand, has been begging and pleading with his father to take his mother out.

James finally decides to follow through and invite Marlene out to dinner. She willingly accepts his invitation for a romantic evening of fine dining and ballroom dancing. This will be their first official date since their divorce and their four years of no contact. James decides to wear his olive-green Martin Greenfield custom-tailored suit. It nicely complements his brown skin tone and slender physique. He is hoping to make a lasting impression on the love of his life.

Marlene has no idea that James is seriously thinking about asking for her hand in marriage at this time. Though she has often dreamed about the three of them being one family again, her primary focus has been on her son. However, she is very pleased with the amount of time that James has been spending with

Jamaal, and she is looking forward to spending an evening out on the town with her ex-husband.

James arrives at Marlene's house, pulls into the driveway, and puts the car in park. He can't wait to see the look on Marlene's face when she finds out that he is taking her to the five-star restaurant where he took her on their very first date, over fifteen years ago. He wants it to be a surprise. However, he is very nervous. He tries hard to contain his nervousness and excitement as he exits the car, with a bouquet of assorted roses in hand. He takes a deep breath to calm himself as he slowly approaches the door and rings the bell.

"I'll get it, Mom," cries Jamaal. He rushes through the living room, swings open the door with great excitement, and gives his dad a big hug. Barely taking breaths between sentences, he excitedly exclaims, "Hey, Dad! Mom is ready. And Dad, she looks great!" With raised eyebrow, he snappily states, "And you look nice too. That's a sharp suit. I know that you and Mom are going to have a wonderful time!" Jamaal is overjoyed by the fact that his father has finally asked his mother out on a date.

James smiles as he gently places his hand on Jamaal's shoulder, in an attempt to calm him down a bit. He gazes at his son and lovingly replies, "Yes, I'm sure that your mom and I will have a wonderful time this evening as we reminiscence about life." James places the crystal vase with the bouquet of assorted roses on the dining room table. He then follows Jamaal into the family room to wait for Marlene.

Jamaal can hardly contain his enthusiasm, as he repeatedly taps his dad on the shoulder. "Dad, Mom has been looking forward to going out! She has been in such a good mood lately, singing and dancing around the house. All she has been able to talk about has been you and how wonderful you are." Jamaal begins to whisper as he pleads with his dad. "But Dad, please don't tell

Mom that I told you that." He places his hand over his mouth while sheepishly whispering under his breath. "She will *kill* me."

"I won't say a word," whispers James. He smiles as he pretends to zip his lips. "My lips are sealed."

"Dad, she even talked about how the two of you first met. She told me all about the restaurant you took her to on your first date. She said it was a very expensive restaurant with live jazz. She went on and on about how the two of you danced the night away as if you were the only two people in the restaurant."

James smiles as he recalls the evening. "Son, she's right. Your mom's absolutely right."

Jamaal pauses as he looks up intently at his dad. "Dad, I know Mom really misses you. Do you think that the two of you will get back together?" he earnestly asks.

"Son, I would like that very much," James assures him. "But you never know. You never know what God has in store for your life. All we can do is hope and pray that it might happen, and I'm hoping that it will happen sooner rather than later."

"Oh, Dad, that would be great!"

"Yes, it would, son. It certainly would," James muses. He gazes at his son with a deep sense of love and admiration.

Marlene loves dressing up. She looks astonishing in her dazzling, gold-laced cocktail dress with Christian Louboutin high-heel pumps and matching purse. She slowly descends the stairs and heads toward the family room where Jamaal and his dad are talking and laughing with each other. She stands quietly at the door while admiring the bond that has developed between the two of them. Marlene smiles as she playfully clears her throat in an attempt to get their attention. "Okay, what are you guys up to?" she coyly asks.

"Oh nothing," says James with a chuckle. "Nothing's going on. We were just having a little father-son chat. That's all."

Marlene sarcastically replies with a smile, "Yeah, right!"

"Wow, you look absolutely gorgeous!" James is mesmerized by Marlene's beauty.

Marlene blushes as she confidently and smugly replies, "Why, thank you. You guys make me feel like I'm on cloud nine. Receiving a compliment from the two men that I love the most is all that matters. No one else's opinion matters, as far as I'm concerned." Marlene lovingly looks up at James as she then clarifies. "Well, except for God's, of course."

"Mom, you really do look great, and I hope you and Dad have a wonderful time!" states Jamaal, giving his mother a great big hug.

"I'm sure we will, son. Your grandmother will be stopping by shortly to take you out to eat and to see the play that you've been dying to see; the classic *Jitney*, by your all-time favorite playwright, August Wilson." Marlene gently pats Jamaal on the back while playfully stating, "No need to wait up for us. I'll see you in the morning." She winks at Jamaal as she reaches for her shawl.

Jamaal looks on as his mother and father walk toward the front door. As they reach it, he calls out, "Good night, Mom. Good night, Dad."

"Good night, son," James replies as he opens the door for Marlene.

Marlene replies in like manner, "Good night, dear."

After seeing his parents off, Jamaal races upstairs to call his grandmother to let her know that his parents have left for dinner.

James is very excited about his plans for the evening. He is beaming from ear to ear as he opens the car door for Marlene. He reaches for her shawl while flirtatiously stating, "Marlene, you will *never* guess where I plan to take you for dinner."

Several thoughts race through Marlene's mind. She knows James well and suspects that he may be taking her to the restaurant that he took her to on their very first date. However, she chooses not to guess, so she replies with a warm smile, "No, dear, I have no idea."

The grin on James's face grows as he closes Marlene's car door. "Well, you're going to be surprised," he confidently states.

As they get close to the area where the restaurant is located, Marlene begins to act surprised. "Oh, James, you didn't! You mean you're taking me—"

James abruptly interrupts her. "Yes, I told you that you'd be surprised!" He chortles with glee.

Marlene is blushing as she thinks about how she has always admired James's chivalry and highly romantic nature. "Wow, I haven't been here since our first date," she proudly proclaims.

"Well, that's good," states James as he reaches for her hand. "That means your last memory of being here was when we were here together all those years ago."

"Hmm, I never thought about it like that, but you are so right," replies Marlene with a modest smile as she reflects on their very first date. "My one and only memory is of us having such a wonderful time talking, laughing, and dancing the night away," she recalls while gazing lovingly at James.

"Well, here we are once again," James says happily. He pulls up to the valet kiosk and hands the car key to the attendant. He then briskly walks around to the passenger side, opens the door, and reaches for Marlene's hand. He gently kisses the back of her hand, pronouncing, "I hope this evening is even more special."

Marlene has no idea what James has planned for the evening. But she confidently replies, "I'm sure it will be," as she daintily exits the car.

James drapes Marlene's shawl across her shoulders as they walk toward the restaurant. They greet the hostess and she escorts them to their private table, which has a breathtaking view of the city. James orders a bottle of the most expensive nonalcoholic sparkling champagne as they peruse the menu.

It is apparent that James and Marlene thoroughly enjoy spending time together. The tone of the conversation becomes increasingly more serious and focused as they begin to talk about their relationship.

After finishing their meal, they order their favorite desserts and delight in sharing them. Then James takes Marlene's hand and softly states, "Marlene, I'm so grateful to God that you are available and are so open to giving me a second chance. One of the reasons I didn't call sooner than I did was because I was so afraid of being rejected or disappointed by the fact that you might have fallen in love and remarried. I couldn't bear the thought of you remarrying, not to mention the thought of Jamaal having a stepfather." James pauses as he thinks about how long they have been separated. Marlene could easily have remarried if she'd wanted to. "However, in knowing you, I know that if you had remarried, he would have been a man of integrity and the best person for you and our son."

Marlene values the institution of marriage and knows that it was God who kept her from desiring a new relationship. She then begins to think about Jamaal, as she firmly declares, "James, my number-one priority has been providing for Jamaal. And to be frank with you, the thought of remarrying never crossed my mind." As Marlene begins to think about all that she and Jamaal have been through over the past couple of years, she looks at James sternly and tells him adamantly, "Mind you, my focus over the past eight years has been on trying to be the best mother *and* father that I could be to our son in the absence of his true father. However, I thank God that he didn't see fit to have me remarry, which helped me to remain open to your coming back into our lives."

James appreciates Marlene's firm and direct, yet warm and loving nature, which helps him to know exactly where she stands. He is quite pleased that she is open to the possibility of reuniting as a family, and he continues the conversation. "Marlene, I am thoroughly convinced that I was temporarily insane when the talk of divorce came up. If I had been thinking straight at the time, I would have never let you go and taken the chance of losing you forever." James gently takes Marlene's hand while looking her squarely in the face. "Marlene, I *promise* that I will make up for lost time with you and our precious little boy," he says confidently.

Marlene believes in James, and she knows that he is sincere in wanting nothing but the best for her and Jamaal. In an attempt to lighten the mood, she says amiably, "Well, he's not such a *little boy* anymore, and I accept. But let me caution you to never make a promise that you cannot keep," she adds.

James smiles at Marlene's gentle, yet firm, take-charge attitude. "Yes, I know better." He warmly looks into Marlene's eyes while reflecting on her spirituality. He then begins to think about his own spiritual growth and development as he comments, "Marlene, you're not going to believe this, but I was re-baptized about three years ago."

Marlene is very excited to learn that James has been focusing on his spiritual growth and development during their time apart. However, she is somewhat surprised that he actually took measures to be re-baptized. She incredulously responds, "James, really? Are you serious? When we were together, you never seemed to have much time for church."

"Yes, I know," replies James. "My focus was on working and making money, but things have changed." He goes on to share how he was reintroduced to church and Christ during their time apart. "What happened was that I was working very closely with a brother in Christ on my job, and he invited me to attend church with him. I accepted his invitation and ended up joining his church about a week later."

"James, that's wonderful! Wow, that is *so good* to hear!" Marlene enthusiastically replies.

"Yes, it was a big step, and it seemed to make all the difference in the world," James confirms with a smile. "It was through my fellowship and contact with members of the church that I began to rethink my priorities."

"You do seem to be more into service now, more so than you have ever been, and that is good to see," states Marlene as she reflects on James's spiritual growth. While they were married, she had often wondered why James did not take a strong interest in church despite his professed faith and belief in God. Marlene lets out a calming sigh. She then solemnly states, "But James, I just hate it that church was not a significant part of your life when we were married."

"Deep down I wanted to make church a significant part of my life. However, I could tell that you were at a different level spiritually, and it just seemed to add to my feelings of insecurity," James thoughtfully enlightens her. "Your life seemed to be so perfect, and me, I just seemed to be so flawed." James sighs while looking off to the side. "Please do not take this the wrong way, but attending church with you left me feeling guilty and very much aware of all the work that I needed to do on myself."

Marlene is troubled by what she is hearing. She thinks, *This is something that James and I could have worked through—if he had only trusted me enough to share his true feelings and vulnerabilities.* In realizing that they could have avoided all the pain and heartache of the past eight years, she passionately cries out, "James, I can't believe what I'm hearing! You know that you could have talked to me about anything, and I do mean anything." Marlene slowly shakes her head from side to side while asking, "Is that not true?"

James remains silent as he gives his ex-wife his undivided attention.

Marlene pauses while reflecting on their marriage: *My God, if we had fought past our fears and openly talked about our vulnerabilities, we could have savaged our marriage.*

In understanding and appreciating Marlene's passion when it comes to their relationship and the family, James calmly states, "Sweetheart, at the time, I just couldn't see it making a difference. There was too much work that I needed to do within myself." James pauses as he warmly gazes into Marlene's eyes. "However, all that has changed. I needed time to find myself. Believe me, I'm a new person."

Marlene's mood softens as she replies, "Yes, that I do know. However, I loved you just the way you were. I just wish we had kept in touch."

"Thank you, Marlene," James states as he breathes a sigh of relief. "I am so happy to hear that. But I'm glad that I have been born again, and nothing or no one is more important to me than the Lord. I have truly learned what it means to put God first in all things, including my personal life."

Marlene smiles inwardly, remaining silent, as she listens to her ex-husband with great love, pride, respect, and admiration.

"When we were together, I know that you would constantly reference your faith and the role that God played in your life. Now, don't get me wrong, I greatly admired and respected that about you, but I didn't quite understand it at the time. However, in meeting and interacting with other born-again believers, I learned that I was not the only person going through the pain that I was experiencing at the time, and it helped to know that." James pauses as he thinks about his spiritual growth. "I learned so much about myself, and it helped to know that other brothers felt the same way that I did before truly accepting Christ into their lives." James smiles at Marlene while lightheartedly stating, "You know—what the average Christian refers to as being *sold out*, or should I say *born again*?"

Marlene smiles as she warmly stares at James, giving him her undivided attention.

James pauses, with his eyes fixed on Marlene. "Marlene, to be honest with you, I never really knew what it meant to be a born-again believer, until recently. I would watch you and just admire your love and commitment to God, but I never really knew what it meant to accept Jesus Christ as Lord and Savior of my life."

Marlene continues to smile at James.

James is smitten by Marlene's beauty as he admires her smile and looks deeply into her eyes. He continues to share. "I truly do thank you for allowing me to be me and not pressuring me to be more than I was able to be at the time. Your faith, gentle spirit, and love for the Lord are the qualities that I love and respect most about you. There were times when I would look at you, and it was almost as though I could see God in you. You would have a glow on your face, and that million-dollar smile would light up the room." James pauses as he thinks about how much he has grown over the past four years. "I know the divorce was hard on you, but I thank you for allowing me the time and space that I needed to find myself."

Marlene appreciates James's honesty and his openness in sharing his true feelings. She comments, "Well, since you brought it up, I guess I can confess that I honestly never stopped praying for you, and I do thank God for answering *our* prayers. And I thank you for sharing and being so open." Marlene attempts to lighten the mood with her sharp, yet playful tone. "And you know what?" she asks. Marlene silently awaits his reply.

James cannot tell whether she is in a serious or joking mood. He has no idea what Marlene is going to say next, so he cautiously replies, "No, I'm afraid I don't know," and waits with bated breath.

Sensing this, Marlene decides to remain serious as she openly confesses her love. "James, I trust you know that I do still love you very much and sincerely welcome you home with open arms."

James lets out the breath he was holding as he reflects on Marlene's bravery in sharing her feelings. He has always appreciated her ability to be very open and honest, no matter what the cost. However, he is not sure where she is going with the conversation, so he chooses to remain silent while giving her his undivided attention as he waits to hear what she has to say next.

Marlene pauses as she notices James's growing smile. She takes that as a cue to continue sharing. "You may not believe this, but to be honest, I never once thought of remarrying. However, I also know deep down in my heart that God is the one responsible for putting our family back together. That's what I love most about the Lord—His unconditional love for us and His wisdom in knowing what's best for each of us, no matter how many mistakes we may make in trying to get it right. God is faithful and just in forgiving us, and therefore, it is up to us to forgive one another."

James is delighted to hear his ex-wife speak of her love for him and faith in God. He leans over to fully embrace her for the first time since their divorce. "Marlene, I love you so much. With God as my witness, I never once stopped loving you. And now that I have you back in my arms, I don't plan to ever let you go."

Marlene gently kisses James on the cheek. She reassures him with great love and affection as she declares, "James, you know that I trust and believe in you totally and completely, and I will continue to trust and believe in you, as you continue to trust and believe in God. You truly are the best thing that has ever happened to me. I thank God for the time that he has allowed us to spend together." Marlene's smile broadens as she reflects on her love for James while lightheartedly adding, "And now that I'm back in your arms, I can honestly say that I never wish to be let go *ever again*—not even to go to work, for that matter."

James smiles while thinking to himself, *This is the perfect time to pop the question.* Thoughts of Marlene saying "no" begin to race through his mind as he nervously reaches into his pocket for the diamond wedding band that he purchased several years ago. He reaches for Marlene's left hand while looking her in the eyes. "Marlene, I have something to ask you," he softly states.

Marlene has no idea that James is about to propose remarriage. She casually replies, "Sure—what is it, my dear?"

"Marlene, I know that we have been divorced for over eight years." James gently kisses the palm of her hand and states, "And I know that I neglected to keep in touch with you and our dearly beloved son. Please know that I do apologize for that."

Marlene has never been one to hold a grudge. She forgave James long before he reinitiated contact with the family. She does not know what James is up to, and her mood shifts as she becomes concerned about his ability to forgive himself. She has a serious look on her face when she tells him, "Oh, James, I forgave you a long time ago. Please know that I do understand—"

James's anxiety around popping the question causes him to politely interrupt Marlene. A thousand thoughts are racing through his mind. "Yes, Marlene, I know," he tells her. "And I deeply appreciate your forgiving me and accepting me back into your life. Your unconditional love for me is truly unbelievable, and I thank God for blessing me with such a dynamic wife."

Marlene smiles as she begins to suspect that James is up to something. He is nervously rubbing the base of her wedding-ring finger, which reminds her of the day he first proposed marriage. She begins to suspect that James is preparing to propose for the second time. However, she remains silent, staring into James's eyes as he lovingly gazes back at her.

James takes a deep breath and prepares to pop the question. "Marlene, I know that it has been a little over a year since our reunion and initial phone conversation, and I have thoroughly enjoyed spending time with both you and Jamaal, but there is something that I need to ask you."

Marlene places her right hand on top of James's hand. "Yes, you have my undivided attention," she softly states.

James fights past his nervousness as he thinks to himself, *It's now or never!* "Marlene, will you be my bride again?" he asks in a near whisper.

Marlene's heart drops, and she takes a deep breath. She is smiling from ear to ear as she responds with great enthusiasm, "Oh, James, as you know, the answer is *yes!* I would love to be your bride again." Marlene leans in to embrace James as tears begin to roll down her cheeks. "James, you have just made me the happiest person in the world for the second time," she tells him through her sniffles.

James is relieved and quite pleased by Marlene's enthusiastic reply. He gently wipes the tears from her eyes and wraps his arms around her, as his mind flashes back to the first time he proposed to her and how excited she was on that day. However, he never imagined that she would respond with such emotion and enthusiasm the second time around. While continuing to embrace Marlene, he warmly expresses, "Marlene, you have just made me the happiest man on the face of the earth. I promise you that I will not let my foolish pride come between us ever again. I wholeheartedly promise you that, with God as my witness!"

Marlene smiles as she looks into James's eyes. She remains silent as tears begin to flow from her eyes.

James leans over to kiss Marlene on the cheek. "Marlene,

sweetheart, I love you," he softly whispers in her ear as he inconspicuously wipes the tears from his own eyes.

Marlene gently kisses James on the lips for the first time since their divorce. She informs him, "Yes, and I love you. Always have and always will."

James smiles as he excitedly states, "All we need to do now is set the date!"

"Whoa! Hold up—not quite!" Marlene jokingly states with a smile, still wiping the tears from her eyes.

James is caught off guard by Marlene's reply. He remains silent while anxiously awaiting her next remark.

Marlene realizes that James is taking her comment very seriously, so she gently grabs his hand. "Hey, what's up with the serious look?" she playfully asks. Her smile broadens as she reassures him, "All is well. I was just thinking that we'd better share the wonderful news with our son and your soon-to-be-once-again mother-in-law before moving forward in setting the date."

James is relieved to know that his proposal has been fully accepted and she plans to move forward in setting a date. He excitedly exclaims, "Wow, you are so right!" The grin on James's face widens as he lightheartedly concludes, "Marlene you are *always* so right, and that's what makes you so special. And I love you for it!"

"We'll be reuniting as a family, so we'll have to share the good news with your son and soon-to-be once again mother-in-law," Marlene playfully states with a smile. "It's no longer just the two of us. But I know that they will both be jumping for joy." Marlene pauses as she thinks about the instrumental role her mother has taken in helping Jamaal deal with the hurt that he has experienced. She then comments, "Mom may be a little concerned, knowing the pain and heartache that the divorce caused me and Jamaal. However, she has always been very open and understanding, and she has fully embraced my decisions in the past. All things considered, I know that she'll be quite pleased with our decision to remarry."

In respecting the newly formed bond that he has established with Marlene, their son, and her mother, James confides, "Marlene, I tell you what, I would like to be the one to share the news with Jamaal and your mother, if that's all right with you. It would be good for them to hear it from me. You've done your share and then some. It's time for me to step up to the plate."

Marlene smiles as she reflects on how good it is going to be to have James back in their lives. She watches him intently while remaining silent.

James looks deeply into her eyes and firmly asserts, "Marlene, trust me when I say that I will not let anything or anybody, including my foolish pride, come between the three of us ever again. I value family life, and I am looking forward to us reuniting as a family. I just regret that I allowed so many years to pass without making contact with you and my—I mean *our*—son. I could have spent those years with the two people who I love more than anything in this whole wide world." James pauses as he reflects on his love for the Lord and clarifies. "Well, that is excluding God, of course." James smiles as he feels the warmth of Marlene's smile and thinks about how much he loves his wife, his family, and his Lord and Savior, Jesus Christ.

"Yes James, I do understand, and I know that we will have plenty of time to spend together as a family. However, given the fact that tomorrow is not promised, I plan to treat each day as if it were our last. I plan to make sure that I'm available to both my—I mean *our*—son and my dearly beloved husband-to-be," she firmly states with a smile.

"Marlene, you are so sweet, and I thank you for being such a loving woman of God," James replies. He is excited about sharing the good news with Jamaal and Marlene's mother. He looks down at his watch and cries out, "Oh my, it's getting late. I hate to see this evening come to an end, but I'm afraid it must. Your mom will be dropping Jamaal off soon, and it would be great if we could share the wonderful news with them this evening."

"Yes, I agree," Marlene lovingly states. She reaches for her purse as they prepare to leave the restaurant.

James helps Marlene with her shawl as they head toward the door.

"James, thank you for making this an unforgettable evening," Marlene says as she gently kisses him on the cheek.

"You're most welcome, and I thank you *and* God for making this evening possible," replies James with a smile as he escorts Marlene to the car. He opens the car door and lovingly states, "God truly does answer prayers, and I thank Him for allowing us to be reunited in love."

Marlene remains silent as she looks up at James with great love and admiration.

Feeling the same way, James returns her gaze. "Marlene, you are and will forever be flesh of my flesh and bone of my bone," he warmly states, "and that which God brings together for His purpose and for His glory let no man put asunder."

Marlene softly smiles as she confidently responds, "And to God be the glory for the great and mighty things that He has done, is doing, and will continue to do in our lives, from this time forth, forevermore."

James looks Marlene in the eyes while stating with conviction, "Marlene, sweetheart, I love you. I honor you. I cherish and adore you and only you. And I will always love you with every fiber of my being, from this day forward, until death do us part."

Marlene smiles as she affirms James's words of love and devotion by nodding her head. She then looks him in the eyes and adds in a soft whisper, "Amen."

James watches as Marlene gracefully settles into the passenger seat and buckles her seat belt. He leans in and gives her a kiss on the cheek as he prepares to gently close her car door. James briskly walks to the other side of the car, settles into the driver's seat, buckles his seat belt, and drops the convertible top on his Maserati GranTurismo. He reaches for Marlene's hand, lovingly staring into her big brown eyes while allowing the expression on his face to speak for itself.

Marlene returns the look as she reflects on the evening and what their new life as one, reunited in love, will be like in spirit and truth.

James prepares to drive off into the night with the stars shining bright.

This concludes phase I of Jamaal's heartrending and at times tumultuous journey to love and be loved, as introduced by Keyana's mother and enjoyed by readers of all ages. Keyana is very pleased with the way the story has ended, and she has a better understanding of what it means to love and be loved by the important people in life. This understanding will serve to guide her in her relationships with her classmates, friends, peers, parents, teachers, and other adult authority figures as she grows and matures. At the same time, it will keep her heart open to love, acceptance, forgiveness, and reconciliation.

EPILOGUE

REFLECTIONS ON THE ART OF
LOVE AND FORGIVENESS

We are admonished to love the Lord our God with all our hearts, our souls, our minds, and our strength. Jesus tells us that this is the greatest commandment issued by God. The second is to love our neighbors as ourselves. So it is in this order: first we must love God, then we must love ourselves, and then we should ideally love our neighbors as we love ourselves. It is the love we have for ourselves that we are to extend to our neighbors. Thus, our individual and collective goal is to love ourselves so that we can, in turn, truly love our neighbors as we love ourselves. This means that we learn how to love and embrace all of who we are—the good, the bad, and the proverbial ugly (according to the common expression). That enables us to consequently love others for who they are and as they are. I am of the belief that when we feel loved, cared for, and forgiven by both God and ourselves, we are more likely to love, care for, and forgive others. The ability to love others truly and sincerely is a beautiful thing, and the ability to love others unconditionally paves the way for forgiveness.

In understanding love, we are reminded in 1 Corinthians Chapter 13 that love does not envy nor rejoice in iniquity but rejoices in the truth. For love never fails and is indeed the greatest gift that we can give to ourselves and one another. God, in His infinite wisdom, knew that we would need to learn how to *love* from the depths of our hearts while also learning how to truly *forgive* from the heart, even when we have been hurt and/or disappointed by the ones who we are struggling to love and/or forgive. God demonstrated His love for us by sending His only begotten Son into the world to reconcile us back to Him. This magnanimous and providential act provides us with a tangible point of reference for both love and forgiveness, in that Jesus represents, and is, the epitome of God's love and forgiveness.

Since God intentionally loves us unconditionally and forgives us of our sins and trespasses, we should be intentional when it comes to loving Him with all our hearts, minds, souls, and strength, while striving to love our neighbors as ourselves. When praying the prayer that Jesus taught His disciples, commonly referred to as The Lord's Prayer, we are asking God to forgive us of our sins, debts, and trespasses in the same manner in which we are willing to forgive others, with the implication being that we are consciously agreeing to let go of anger, bitterness, and resentment toward others. Therefore it is incumbent upon us to learn how to truly *love* ourselves and others, just as it is incumbent upon us to learn how to *forgive* ourselves and others, if we do indeed desire to be blessed by God.

We have been given the *gift of love*, along with the *gift of forgiveness*, by our heavenly Father, which enables us to love and forgive each other. Thus let us begin to practice the *art* of love and forgiveness, so that we may receive the blessings and the inheritance that our Father has in store for us, in spirit and truth. As we free ourselves to the point where we are able to truly forgive ourselves and others, we simultaneously allow ourselves the freedom to begin to heal from the pain caused by our own offenses as well as those of others. When choosing to consciously hold a grudge against another person, we must bear in mind that no one is perfect. For we all have our shortcomings and are quite prone to make mistakes several times over. Hopefully we do not repeat the same mistakes, because we do need to learn from our errant ways while seeking to better ourselves in the process.

Just as we can *choose* to hold a grudge, we can also *choose* to love and forgive. Jesus summarizes this point very nicely in the Gospel of Matthew, Chapter 5, verses 44-48, wherein He explains how we are to treat those who mistreat us. Eugene Peterson, in *The Message: The Bible, in Contemporary Language*, puts it this way: "You're familiar with the old written law, 'Love your friend,' and its unwritten companion, 'Hate your enemy.' I'm challenging that. I'm telling you to love your enemies. Let them bring out the best in you, not the worst. When someone gives you a hard time, re-spond with the energies of prayer, for then you are working out of your true selves, your God-created selves. This is what God does. He gives his best—the sun to warm and the rain to nourish—to everyone, regardless: the good and bad, the nice and nasty. If all you do is love the lovable, do you expect a bonus? Anybody can do that. If you simply say hello to those who greet you, do you expect a medal? Any run-of-the-mill sinner does that. In a word, what I'm saying is, 'Grow up. You're kingdom subjects. Now live like it. Live out your God-created identity. Live generously and graciously toward others, the way God lives toward you.'"

In closing, I encourage you to be intentional in demonstrat-ing true acts of love and forgiveness toward one another, while bearing in mind that love truly is kind and long-suffering. As you do so, I pray that God will continue to bless and keep you all the days of your life and cause His Face to shine ever so brightly upon you and your loved ones as you experience His glorious presence and power operating in your life. As you find it in your heart to

Printed in the United States
By Bookmasters